Carol from Daddy

Carol.
Xmas 194?

Dr. Possum told Sammie he would have to stay in
until his leg was better. (*See page* 17.)

UNCLE WIGGILY
AND
THE LITTLETAILS

By

HOWARD R. GARIS

AUTHOR OF

Uncle Wiggily's Picture Book, Uncle Wiggily's
Story Book, Uncle Wiggily's Adventures,
Uncle Wiggily's Automobile, etc.

ILLUSTRATED BY ELMER RACHE

UNCLE WIGGILY
Reg. U. S. Pat. Off:

•NEW•YORK•
'THE•PLATT•&•MUNK•C̲o̲ INC•

PUBLISHER'S NOTE

The stories herein contained appeared originally in the Evening News, of Newark, N. J., where (so many children and their parents have been kind enough to say) they gave pleasure to a number of little folks and grown-ups also. Permission to issue the stories in book form was kindly granted by the publisher and editor of the News, to whom the author extends his thanks.

CONTENTS

7

8 Contents

Uncle Wiggily and the Littletails

STORY I

SAMMIE LITTLETAIL IN A TRAP

ONCE upon a time there lived in a small house built underneath the ground two curious little folk, with their father, their mother, their uncle and Miss Jane Fuzzy-Wuzzy. Jane Fuzzy-Wuzzy was the nurse, hired girl and cook, all in one, and the reason she had such a funny name was because she was a funny cook. She had long hair, a sharp nose, a very long tail and the brightest eyes you ever saw. She could stay under water a long time, and was a fine swimmer. In fact, Miss Jane Fuzzy-Wuzzy was a big muskrat, and the family she worked for was almost as strange as she was.

There was Papa Littletail, Mamma Littletail, Sammie Littletail, Susie Littletail and Uncle Wiggily Longears. The whole family had very

long ears and short tails; their eyes were rather
pink and their noses used to twinkle, just like
the stars on a frosty night. Now you have
guessed it. This was a family of bunny rabbits,
and they lived in a nice hole, which was called a
burrow. This hole they had dug under ground
in a big park on the top of a mountain, back of
Orange. Not the kind of oranges you eat, you
know, but the name of a place, and a very nice
place, too, in New Jersey.

After Uncle Wiggily became a very rich rabbit gentleman he bought a fine, hollow stump
bungalow for the family, as you probably have
heard. There was a radio in the bungalow and a
telephone and many other things. But, for the
present, Uncle Wiggily and Nurse Jane lived
in an underground burrow.

In spite of her strange name, and the fact that
she was a muskrat, Nurse Jane Fuzzy-Wuzzy
was a very good cook and quite kind to the children bunnies, Sammie and Susie. Besides looking after them, Miss Fuzzy-Wuzzy used to
sweep the burrow, make up the beds of leaves and
grass, and go to market to get bits of carrots,
turnips or cabbage, which last Sammie and
Susie liked better than ice cream.

Uncle Wiggily Longears was an elderly rabbit, who had the rheumatism, and he could not

do much. Sometimes, when Miss Fuzzy-Wuzzy
was very busy, he would go after the cabbage or
turnips for her. Uncle Wiggily Longears was
a wise rabbit, and as he had no other home, and
was not married, as yet, Papa Littletail let him
stay in a warm corner of the burrow. To pay for
his board the little bunnies' uncle would give
them lessons in how to behave. One day, after
he had told them how needful it was to always
have two holes, or doors, to your burrow, so that
if a dog chased you in one hole, you could go out
of the other hole, Uncle Wiggily said:

"Now, children, I think that is enough for one
day, so you may go out and have some fun in the
snow."

But first Jane Fuzzy-Wuzzy looked out of
the back door, and then she looked out of the
front door, to see that there were no dogs or
hunters about. Then Sammie and Susie crept
out. They had lots of fun, and pretty soon, when
they were a long way from home, they saw a hole
in the ground. In front of it was a nice, juicy
cabbage stalk.

"Look!" cried Sammie. "Miss Fuzzy-Wuzzy
must have lost that cabbage on her way home
from the store!"

"That hole isn't the door to our house," said
Susie.

"Yes it is," insisted Sammie, "and I am going to eat the cabbage. I didn't have much breakfast, and I'm hungry."

"Be careful," whispered Susie. "Uncle Wiggily Longears warned us to look on all sides before we ate any cabbage we found."

"I don't believe there's any danger," spoke Sammie. "I'm going to eat it," and he went right up to the cabbage stalk.

But Sammie did not know that the cabbage stalk was part of a trap, put there to catch animals. No sooner had he taken a bite, than there suddenly sounded a click, and Sammie felt a terrible pain in his left hind leg.

"Oh, Susie!" he cried out. "Oh, Susie! Something has caught me by the leg! Run home, Susie, as fast as you can, and tell papa!"

Susie was so frightened that she began to cry, but, as she was a brave little rabbit girl, she started off toward the underground house. When she got there she jumped right down the front door hole, and called out:

"Oh, mamma! Oh, papa! Sammie is caught! He went to bite the cabbage stalk, and he is caught in a horrible trap!"

"Caught!" exclaimed Uncle Wiggily Longears. "Sammie caught in a trap! That is too bad! We must rescue him at once. Come on!"

he called to Papa Littletail, and, though Uncle Wiggily Longears was quite lame with the rheumatism, he started off with Sammie's papa, and next, if your radio doesn't talk in its sleep and awaken the vacuum sweeper, I will tell you how they saved the little boy rabbit.

STORY II

SAMMIE LITTLETAIL IS RESCUED

WHEN Uncle Wiggily Longears and Papa Littletail hurried from the underground house to rescue Sammie, Mamma Littletail was much frightened. She nearly fainted, and would have done so completely, only Nurse Jane Fuzzy-Wuzzy brought her some parsnip juice which made her feel better.

"Oh, hurry and get my little boy out of that trap!" cried Mamma Littletail, when she could speak again. "Do you think he will be much hurt, Uncle Wiggily?"

"Oh, no; not much," Mr. Longears said. "I was caught in a trap once when I was a young rabbit, and I got over it. Only I caught a dreadful cold, from being kept out in the rain all night. We will bring Sammie safely home to you."

While Uncle Wiggily Longears and Papa Littletail were on their way to the rescue, poor Sammie, left all alone in the woods, with his left hind foot caught in a cruel trap, felt very lonely indeed.

14

"I'll never take any more cabbage without looking all around it, to see if there is a trap near it," he said to himself. "No indeed I will not," and then he tried to pull himself out of the trap, but could not.

Pretty soon Sammie saw his father and his uncle coming over the snow toward him, and he felt much better.

"Now we must be very careful," said Uncle Wiggily Longears, to Papa Littletail. "There may be more traps about."

So Uncle Wiggily sat upon his hind legs, and Papa Littletail sat up on his hind legs, and they both made their noses twinkle like stars on a very frosty night. For that is the way rabbits smell, and these two were wise bunnies, who could smell a trap as far as you can smell perfumery. They could not, this time, smell any more traps with their noses, and they could not see any more traps with their pink eyes, so they hopped quite close to Sammie, who was held fast by his left hind leg in the trap into which he had stepped by accident.

"Does it hurt you very much?" asked his papa, and he put his front paws around his little rabbit boy, and gave him a good hug.

"Not very much, papa," replied Sammie, bravely, "but I wish I was out."

"We'll soon have you out," said Uncle Wiggily Longears. Then, with his strong hind feet he kicked away the snow and dried leaves from the trap. Sammie could now see how he had been fooled. The trap was so covered up that only the cabbage stump showed, so it is no wonder that Sammie stepped into the open jaws and was caught.

The two older rabbits tried to get Sammie out, but they could not, because the trap was too strong.

"What shall we do?" asked Papa Littletail, as he sat down and scratched his left ear, which he always did when he was worried about anything.

"The trap is fast to a piece of wood by a chain," said Uncle Wiggily Longears. "We will have to gnaw through the wood, and then take Sammie, the trap, chain and all, to our home. Once there, we can call in Dr. Possum, and he can open the trap and get Sammie's leg out."

So the two big rabbits set to work to gnaw through the wood, to which the chain of the trap was fastened. Sammie Littletail tried not to cry from the pain, but some tears did come, and they froze on his face, close to his little pink nose, for the weather was quite cold.

"I should have given you a lesson about traps," said Uncle Wiggily Longears; "then perhaps

you would not have been caught.   I will give you
a lesson to-morrow, Sammie."

Finally the wood was gnawed through, and
Sammie, with his uncle on one side and his papa
on the other, to help him, reached home.   The
trap was still on his leg, and he could not go very
fast.   In fact, the three of them had to go so
slowly that a hunter and his dog ran after them.
The rabbits managed, however, to jump down
the hole of the underground house just in time,
and the big hunting dog did not get them.   He
soon got tired of waiting, and went away.   Then
Dr. Possum was sent for, and with his strong
tail he quickly opened the trap, and Sammie was
free.   But his leg hurt him very much, and Nurse
Jane Fuzzy-Wuzzy put him in a bed of soft
leaves and gave him some sassafras and elder-
berry tea.   Dr. Possum told Sammie he would
have to stay in the burrow for a week, until his
leg was better.   Sammie did not want to, but his
mother insisted on it.

To-morrow I will tell you an adventure that
happened to Susie Littletail, when she went to
the store for some cabbage.   But please ask the
loaf of bread not to go sliding on the butter plate.
It might slip and crack its crust.

STORY III

WHAT HAPPENED TO SUSIE LITTLETAIL

IT was very lonesome for Sammie Littletail to stay in the underground house for a whole week after he had been caught in the trap. He had to move about on a crutch, which Uncle Wiggily Longears, that wise old rabbit, gnawed out of a piece of cornstalk for him.

"Oh, dear, I wish I could go out and play!" exclaimed Sammie one day. "It's awfully tiresome in here in the dark. I wish I could do something."

"Would you like a nice, juicy cabbage leaf?" asked Susie.

"Wouldn't I, though!" cried Sammie. "But there isn't any in the pantry. I heard Nurse Jane Fuzzy-Wuzzy tell mother so."

"I'll go to the store and get you some," offered his sister. "I know where it is."

The cabbage store was a big field where Farmer Tooker kept his cabbage covered with straw during the winter. It was not far from the burrow, and, though it was not really a store, the

18

rabbits always called it that.   So that was where
Susie Littletail went.   She scraped the snow off
the straw with her hind feet and kicked the straw
away so she could get at the cabbage.   Then
she began to gnaw off the sweetest leaves she
could find for her little sick brother.   She had
broken off quite a number of leaves, and was
thinking how nice they would be for him, when
she suddenly smelled something strange.

It was not cabbage nor turnips nor carrots
that Susie smelled.   Nor was it sweet clover, nor
any smell like that.   It was the smell of danger,
and Susie, like all her family, could smell danger
quite a distance.   This time she knew it was a
man with a dog and a gun who was coming toward her.   For Uncle Wiggily Longears had
told Susie how to know when such a thing happened.

"Oh, it's some of those horrid hunters; I know
it is!" exclaimed Susie.   "I must run home,
though I haven't half enough cabbage."

She took the leaves she had gnawed off in her
mouth and hopped away toward the underground house.   All at once a dog sprang out of
the bushes at Susie and the man with the gun
shot at her, but he did not hit her.   Susie was so
frightened, however, that she dropped the cabbage leaves and ran for her life.

Oh, how fast Susie Littletail ran and hopped. She never ran so fast before in all her life, and, just as the dog was going to grab her, she saw the back door of her house, and down into it she popped like a cork going into a bottle.

"Oh! Oh! Oh!" Susie cried three times, just like that. "I am safe!" and she ran to where her brother was resting on a bed of leaves.

"Why, Susie!" Sammie called to her. "Whatever is the matter?"

"Yes. Why have you been running so?" asked Nurse Jane Fuzzy-Wuzzy. "What happened?"

"A big dog chased me," answered Susie. "But I got away."

"Where is my cabbage?" Sammie wanted to know. "I am so hungry for it."

"Oh, I'm so sorry, but I had to drop it," explained Susie. "Oh, Nurse Jane, is papa home safe? Where is Uncle Wiggily Longears? I hope neither of them is out, for I'm afraid that hunter and his dog will see them."

"Your uncle is asleep in his room," said the muskrat nurse. "His rheumatism hurts him this weather. As for your papa, he has not come home yet, but I guess he is wise enough to keep out of the way of dogs. Now don't make any noise, for your mamma is lying down with a headache. I have a little preserved clover, done up in sugar, put away in the cupboard, and I will give you some."

"That is better than cabbage," declared Sammie, joyfully.

But, just as Nurse Jane Fuzzy-Wuzzy was going to the cupboard to get the sugared clover, something ran down into the underground house. It was a long, thin animal, with a sharp nose, sharper even than Jane Fuzzy-Wuzzy's nose, and when the nurse saw the curious little beast, she cried out in fright.

"Oh, run, children! Run!" she screamed. "This is a very dreadful creature indeed! It is a ferret, but I will drive him out, and he shan't hurt you!"

Then Nurse Jane Fuzzy-Wuzzy, dropping the pan of potatoes she was peeling for supper, sprang at the ferret. And in the next story, you shall hear how Miss Fuzzy-Wuzzy drove the ferret from the underground home and saved the bunny children.

But of course I cannot tell the story if the rice pudding throws its raisins at the coffee pot.

STORY IV

PAPA LITTLETAIL'S PICTURE

WHEN Nurse Jane Fuzzy-Wuzzy called out to the two bunny children to run away from the ferret, Sammie and Susie were so frightened that they hardly knew what to do. Their mother came into the sitting-room of the burrow, from the dark bedroom where she had gone to lie down, because of a headache, and she also was much alarmed. So was Uncle Wiggily Long-ears, who was awakened from his nap by the cries of the nurse.

"Run and hide! Run and hide!" called Miss Fuzzy-Wuzzy, and all the rabbits ran and hid. The ferret, which was a long, slender animal, something like a weasel, had been put into the burrow by the hunter, who stood outside at the back door, hoping the rabbits would run out that way so he could shoot them. But they did not. Instead, they went into the darkest part of the underground house. Nurse Jane Fuzzy-Wuzzy went bravely up to the ferret.

"Now you get right out of this house," she said. "We don't want you here!"

The ferret said nothing, but kept crawling all around, looking for the rabbits. He was careful to keep away from the muskrat, for, in spite of her soft name, Nurse Jane Fuzzy-Wuzzy had very sharp and hard teeth.

"Come on, now; get right out of here!" the nurse ordered again, but the ferret would not go. He wanted to catch the rabbits. Then the musk-rat lady nurse jumped right up on his back and bit him quite hard on one of his little ears. The ferret squealed at this.

Next Miss Fuzzy-Wuzzy nipped him on the other ear; not very hard, you know, but just hard enough to make that ferret wish he had stayed out of the underground house.

"Now will you go?" asked the nurse.

"Yes," said the ferret, "I will," and he turned around and walked right out of the house. The hunter was very much surprised when his ferret appeared without having driven out any rabbits.

"Well," said the hunter, "I guess I made a mistake, but I was sure I saw a rabbit go down that hole. I think I had better be going." So he called his dog, put his ferret into his pocket and went away. And, oh, how glad Sammie and Susie Littletail were!

Pretty soon Papa Littletail came hurrying home. As soon as he entered the burrow the children noticed that he was rather pale. He said that he had had a terrible fright, for, as he was on his way home from Mr. Drake's house, a boy had pointed a big, black thing at him, which clicked like a gun, but did not make a loud noise. Then Susie told her father about the dog who chased her, and how the ferret had frightened them.

"It is a good thing you were not shot," said Mamma Littletail to her husband. "I don't know what we would have done if such a dreadful thing had happened. Boys are terrible."

"I did have a narrow escape," admitted Papa Littletail. "The boy had a sort of square, black box, and I'm sure it was filled with bullets. It had a great, round, shiny eye, that he pointed straight at me, and, when something clicked, he cried out, 'There, I have him!' But I did not seem to be hurt."

"I know what happened to you," said Uncle Wiggily Longears, and he rubbed his leg that had the worst rheumatism in it. "You had your picture taken; that's all."

"My picture taken?" repeated Papa Littletail, as he scratched his left ear, which he always did when he was puzzled.

"That is it," said the children's uncle. "It happened to me once. The boy had a camera, not a gun. It does not hurt to have your picture taken. It is not like being shot."

"Then I wish all hunters would take pictures of us, instead of shooting at us," said Sammie, and Susie, also, thought that would be much nicer. Uncle Wiggily told how lovers of animals often take their pictures, to put in books and magazines, for little boys and girls to look at.

"Well," said Papa Littletail, "I suppose I should be very proud to have my picture taken, but I am not the least bit."

Then he gave Sammie some nice pieces of chocolate-covered turnip, which Mr. Drake had sent to the little boy with the lame leg.

"Do you think I can get out to-morrow?" asked Sammie, after supper. "My leg is quite well."

"I think so," replied his papa. "I will ask Dr. Possum."

Which he did, and Sammie was allowed to go out. He had a very curious adventure, too, and I think I shall tell you about it in the next story if you go to bed early now. Though I wouldn't like to hear that the apple dumpling fell off the table and made crumbs on the gas stove.

STORY V

SAMMIE LITTLETAIL DIGS A BURROW

SAMMIE LITTLETAIL found that his leg was quite well enough to walk on, without the cornstalk crutch, so the day after his papa's picture had been taken, the little rabbit boy started to leave the burrow.

"Come along, Susie," he called to his sister.

"I will also go with you," said Uncle Wiggily Longears. "I will give you children a few lessons in digging burrows. It is time you learned, for some day you will want an underground house of your own."

So Mr. Longears led the little rabbits to a nice place in the big park on top of the mountain, where the earth was soft, and showed Sammie and Susie how to hollow out rooms and halls, how to make back and front doors, and many other things a rabbit should know about burrows.

"I think that will be enough of a lesson today," said Uncle Wiggily, after a while. "We will go home, now."

26

"No," spoke Sammie, "I want to dig some more. It's lots of fun."

"You had better come with us," Susie said.

But Sammie would not, though he promised to be home before dark. So while Uncle Wiggily and Susie Littletail started off, Sammie continued to dig. He dug and he dug and he dug, until he was a long distance under ground, and had really made quite a fine burrow for a little rabbit. All at once he felt a sharp pain in his left front leg.

"Ouch!" Sammie cried. "Who did that?"

"I did," answered a little, furry creature, all curled up in a hole in the ground. "What do you mean by digging into my house? Can't you see where you are going?"

"Of course," answered Sammie, as he looked at his sore leg. "But couldn't you see me coming, and tell me to stop?"

"No, I couldn't see you," was the reply.

"Why not?"

"Why not? Because I'm blind. I'm a mole, and I can't see; but I get along just as well as if I did. Now, I suppose, I've got to go to work and mend the hole you made in the side of my parlor. It's a very large hole."

The mole lived underground, just as the rabbits did, only in a smaller house.

"I'm very sorry," said Sammie.

"That doesn't do much good," spoke the mole, as she began to stop up the hole Sammie had made. She really did very well for a blind animal, but then she had been blind so long that she did not know what daylight looked like. "You had better dig in some other place, little rabbit boy," the mole advised, as she finished stopping up the hole.

Sammie thought so himself, and began digging in a new place. He went quite deep, and when he thought he was far enough down, he began digging upward, so as to come out and make a back door to his furrow, as his uncle had taught him to do.

Sammie dug and he dug and he dug. All at once his feet burst through the soft soil, and he found that he had come out on top of the ground. But what a funny place he was in! It was not at all like the part of the park near his burrow, and he was a little frightened. There were many tall trees about, and in one was a big gray squirrel, who sat up and chattered at the sight of Sammie, as if he had never seen a rabbit before.

"What are you doing here?" asked the squirrel. "Don't you know rabbits are not allowed here?" The squirrel frisked his tail very fast.

"Why not?" asked Sammie.

"Because there are nice trees about, and the keepers of the park fear you and your rabbit family will gnaw the bark off and spoil them."

"We never spoil trees," declared Sammie, though he just then remembered that his Uncle Wiggily had once said something about apple-tree bark being very good to eat.

"There's another reason," went on the squirrel, chattering away.

"What is it?" asked Sammie.

"Look over there and you'll see," was the reply, and when Sammie looked, with his little body half out of the hole he had made, he saw a great animal, with long horns, coming straight at him. He tried to run back down the hole, but he found he had not made it large enough to turn around in.

So Sammie Littletail, frightened as he was at the dreadful animal, had to jump out of the burrow to get ready to run down it again, and, just as he did so, the big animal cried out to him:

"Hold on there!"

Sammie shook with fright, and did not dare move. But, after all, the big animal did not intend to harm him. And what happened, and who the big animal was I will tell you in the next story; if the rubber ball doesn't bounce in the cup of tea and splash it in the face of the clock.

STORY VI

SAMMIE AND SUSIE HELP MRS. WREN

THE big animal with the horns came close to Sammie.

"What are you doing here?" he asked.

"I—I don't know," replied the little rabbit boy. Sammie was puzzled.

"How did you get here?" asked the big animal.

"I was digging a new burrow, and I—I just happened to come out here. But I'll go right away again, if you'll let me," said Sammie.

"Of course I'll let you. Don't you know it's against the rules of the park to be here? What do you suppose they have different parts of the park for, if it isn't to keep you rabbits out of certain places?"

The big animal seemed rather angry and shook his head and horns at the little rabbit boy.

"I'm sure I don't know," was all Sammie could say.

"Do you know who I am?" asked the horned creature.

30

"No—no, sir."

"Well, I'm a deer."

"My—my mother calls me that, sometimes—when I've been real good," said Sammie.

"No, I don't mean that kind at all," and the deer tried to smile. "My name is spelled differently. I'm a cousin of the Santa Claus reindeer. But you must go now. No rabbits are allowed in the part of the park where we live. You should not have come here," and again the deer shook his horns at Sammie.

"I—I never will again," said the little rabbit boy. Then, before the deer knew what was happening, Sammie jumped down his new burrow, ran along to the front door, and darted off toward home.

When he was almost there he saw a little brown bird sitting on a bush, and the bird seemed to be calling to him.

"Wait a minute, little rabbit boy," said the bird. "Why are you in such a hurry?"

"Because I saw such a dreadful animal," was Sammie's reply, and he told about the deer.

"Pooh! Deer are very nice creatures indeed," said the bird. "I used to know one, and I used to perch on his horns. But what I stopped to ask you about was whether you know of a nice nest which I could rent for this Spring. You see, I have come up from the South a little earlier than usual, and I can't find the nest I had last year. It was in a little wooden house that a nice man built for me, but the wind has blown it down. I didn't know but what you might have seen a little nest somewhere."

"No," said Sammie, "I haven't. I am very sorry."

"So am I," went on the little brown bird. "But I must tell you my name. I am Mrs. Wren."

"Oh, I have heard about you," said the little rabbit.

"Are you sure you don't know of a nest about here?" Mrs. Wren asked anxiously. "I don't want to fly all the way back down South. Suppose you go home and ask your mother."

"I will," said Sammie. "Don't you want to come, too?"

"Yes, I think I will. Oh, dear! I'm quite hungry. I declare, I had such an early breakfast, I'm almost starved."

"I know my mother will give you something to eat," said Sammie politely, "that is, if you like cabbage, carrots and such things."

"Oh, yes, almost anything will do. Now, you go ahead, and I will follow."

So Sammie Littletail bounced and hopped on along the ground, and Mrs. Wren flew along overhead in the air like a plane.

"Where do you live?" she asked Sammie.

"In a burrow."

"What is a burrow?" inquired Mrs. Wren.

"Why, it's a house," said Sammie.

"You are mistaken," said the bird, though she spoke politely. "A nest is the only house there is."

"Well, a burrow is our house," declared Sammie. "You'll see."

He was soon home, and, while the bird waited outside, he went in to ask his mother if she knew of a nest Mrs. Wren could rent.

"What a funny question!" said Mamma Littletail. "I will go out and see Mrs. Wren."

So she went out, and the bird asked about a nest. But, as the rabbits never had any use for them, the bunny knew nothing about such things.

"Oh, dear!" exclaimed the bird. "Wherever shall I stay to-night? Oh, what trouble I am in."

"You might stay with us to-night," said Mamma Littletail, kindly, "and look for a nest to-morrow."

"I never lived in a burrow," said Mrs. Wren, "but I will try it," so she flew down into the un-

derground house. Next I am going to tell you
how the wren bird did a great kindness to Uncle
Wiggily. That is I can tell the story if the cake
of soap doesn't use the wash rag for a sail and go
swimming all around the bath tub.

STORY VII

UNCLE WIGGILY GETS SHOT

EARLY the next morning Mrs. Wren, who had spent the night in the burrow home of the Littletail family, got up. She had some cabbage leaves for her breakfast, and then started to leave.

"Where are you going?" asked Susie Littletail.

"I must go hunt for a nest," said the little bird. "You see, I want to begin housekeeping as early as I can this Spring. As there are so many birds coming up from the South, I want to get a house before all the best ones are taken."

So, having thanked Sammie Littletail for showing her the way to the burrow, and also thanking his mamma and papa, the wren bird flew away. She promised, however, to come back if she could not find a place to start housekeeping.

"That Mrs. Wren is a very nice creature indeed," said Mamma Littletail.

"Indeed she is," agreed Papa Littletail, as he started off to work in the carrot store, where he was employed as a bookkeeper.

"It is a nice day," said Uncle Wiggily Long-ears, after a while. "I think I shall go for a walk. It may do my rheumatism good."

"May I come?" asked Sammie; but his uncle said he thought the little boy rabbit should stay home. So Sammie did, and he and Susie found a place where some nice clover was just coming up in a field. They nibbled the sweet leaves.

Just before dinner time Uncle Wiggily Long-ears came limping back to the burrow. He was running and hopping as hard as he could, but that was not very fast.

"Why, Wiggily, whatever has happened?" asked Mrs. Littletail, who had come to the front door to see if her children were all right. "Is your rheumatism worse? Why do you limp so?"

"Because," answered Uncle Wiggily Long-ears, "I have been shot."

"Shot?" cried Mrs. Littletail.

"In the left hind leg," went on Uncle Wiggily. "The same leg that has the rheumatism in it so bad. Oh, dear! I wish you would please send for Dr. Possum."

"I will; right away. Sammie!" Mrs. Littletail called, "go for Dr. Possum, for your uncle. He has been shot. How did it happen, Wiggily?"

"Well, I was down in the swamp, looking for some sassafras root, which Mr. Drake said was good for rheumatism, when a man fired a gun at me. I jumped, but not in time, and several pieces of lead are in my leg."

"Oh, how dreadful!" cried Mamma Littletail.

In a little while Sammie came back with Dr. Possum.

"Ha! This is bad business," spoke the long-tailed doctor, when he looked at Uncle Wiggily's leg. "I fear I shall have to operate."

"Anything, so you get the shot out," said the old rabbit. "Oh, how I suffer!"

Dr. Possum tried to get the leaden pellets out of Uncle Wiggily's leg, but he could not, they were in so deep.

"This is very bad business, indeed," said Dr. Possum. "I fear I shall have to take your leg off."

"Will it hurt?" asked Uncle Wiggily.

"Um-er-well, not very much," said the animal doctor, as he twirled his glasses on his tail.

Just then, who should come into the burrow but Mrs. Wren. She was very much surprised to see Uncle Wiggily lying on a bed of soft grass, with the doctor bending over him.

"What is the matter?" she asked.

"I have been shot," said Uncle Wiggily, "and the doctor cannot get the bullets out."

"Suppose you let me try," said Mrs. Wren. "I have a very sharp bill, and I think I can pull them out."

"Then you are a sort of a doctor," said Uncle Wiggily. "Go ahead, and see what you can do."

"Yes, do," urged Dr. Possum.

So the little brown bird put her beak in the holes in Uncle Wiggily's leg, where the bullets had gone in, and she pulled every one out. It hurt a little, but Uncle Wiggily did not make much of a fuss.

"There," said Mrs. Wren at last, "that is done. They're all out!"

Then Dr. Possum put some salve on the leg and bound it up, promising to come in next day to see how Uncle Wiggily was getting on.

"Did you find a nest-house?" asked Mamma Littletail of the bird.

"No," was the answer, "I think I shall have to stay with you another night, if you will let me. Perhaps I shall find a nest to-morrow."

So she stayed with the Littletail family another night, and in the next story I shall tell you how Mrs. Wren found a nest. But please ask the milk bottle not to turn a somersault on the back steps and scare the loaf of bread.

STORY VIII

SUSIE AND SAMMIE FIND A NEST

SAMMIE LITTLETAIL was up early the next morning. He had not slept very well, for Uncle Wiggily Longears had groaned very much because of the pain in his leg where he was shot. Sammie thought if he got up early, and went for some nice, fresh carrots for his uncle, it would make the old gentleman rabbit feel better.

While Sammie was digging up some carrots, in a field not far from the burrow where he lived, he saw the same gray squirrel that had warned him about not going into the deer park.

"What are you doing now?" asked the squirrel. "It seems to me you are always doing something."

"I am digging carrots for Uncle Wiggily Longears, who was shot," said Sammie.

"That is a very nice thing to do," the gray squirrel said. "You are a better boy rabbit than I thought you were."

"What are you doing here?" Sammie asked the squirrel.

"Me? Oh, I am moving into a new nest. I am getting ready for Spring."

"A new nest!" exclaimed Sammie, and, all at once, he thought of Mrs. Wren, who could not find a nest-house to live in. "What are you going to do with your old nest?" the little boy rabbit asked the squirrel.

"Why leave it, to be sure. I never move my nest."

"Don't you want it any more?"

"Not in the least. I am through with it."

"May I have it?" asked Sammie, very politely.

"You? What can a rabbit do with a nest in a tree? You rabbits live in burrows," said the squirrel.

"I know that," Sammie admitted. "I was not asking for myself," and then he told the squirrel about Mrs. Wren. "May she have your old nest?" he asked.

"Why, yes, if she likes it," the squirrel replied. "Only I am afraid she will find it rather large for such a little bird."

"I will hurry home and tell her," spoke Sammie. "Thanks, a lot, Mrs. Squirrel."

"All right. Tell Mrs. Wren she can move in any time she likes," called the gray squirrel after

Sammie, who, filling his forepaws with carrots, started off toward home as fast as he could run. He found Mamma Littletail getting breakfast, and at once told her the good news. Then he told Mrs. Wren, who had gotten up early to get the early worm that always gets up before the alarm clock goes off.

"I will go and look at the nest at once," said the little bird. "I am very much obliged to you, Sammie. Where is it?"

"Susie and I will show you," spoke the little boy rabbit. "Only we cannot go all the way, because rabbits are not allowed in the deer park. But I can point the nest out to you."

So, after breakfast, Sammie and Susie started off. They ran on the ground and the little brown bird flew along over their heads. She went so much faster than they did that she had to stop every once in a while and wait for them. But at last they got to the place where they could see the deserted squirrel nest.

"There it is," said Sammie, pointing to the tree.

"So I observe," said the bird. "I will fly up and look at it," which she did. She was gone some time, and when she flew back to the ground, where Sammie and Susie were waiting for her, the children asked:

"Did you like it?"

"I think it will do very well," replied Mrs. Wren. "It is a little larger than I need, and there are not the improvements I am used to. There is no hot and cold water and no bathroom, but then, I suppose, I can bathe in the brook, so that is no objection. There is no roof to the nest, though."

"No roof?" repeated Sammie.

"No. You see, squirrels never have a roof such as I am used to, but when my family comes from the South we can build one. I will take the nest, and I hope you bunnies will come to see me sometimes, when I am settled, and have the carpets down."

"We can't climb trees," objected Susie.

"That's so—you can't," admitted Mrs. Wren. "Never mind, I can fly down and see you. Now I think I will begin to clean out the nest, for the squirrels have left a lot of nutshells in it."

So she began to clean out the nest, and Susie and Sammie started home. But, before they got there something happened, and what it was I will tell you, perhaps, in the next story, if the rooster doesn't crow and wake me up before I have time to put a clean dress on the lollypop so it can go to school.

STORY IX

SAMMIE LITTLETAIL FALLS IN

WHEN Sammie Littletail and his sister Susie went off toward their underground house, after they had shown Mrs. Wren where she could get the squirrel's old nest for a home, the little rabbit children felt very happy. They ran along, jumping over stones, leaping through the grass that was beginning to get very green, and had a jolly time.

"I wonder what makes me feel so good?" said Sammie to his sister. "It's just as if Christmas was coming, or something like that; yet it isn't. I don't know what it is."

"I know," spoke Susie, who was very wise for a little bunny-rabbit girl.

"What is it?" asked Sammie, as he paused to nibble at a sweet root that was sticking out of the ground, looking for Spring.

"It is because we have been kind to somebody," went on Susie Littletail. "We did the little

43

brown wren bird a kindness in showing her the
squirrel's old nest where she could go to housekeeping, and that's what makes us happy."

"Are you sure?" asked Sammie.

"Yes," said Susie; "I am," and she sat up on
her hind legs and sniffed the air to see if there
was any danger about. "You always feel good
when you do any one a kindness," Susie went
on. "Once I wanted to go out and play, and I
couldn't, because Nurse Jane Fuzzy-Wuzzy was
away and mamma had a headache. So I stayed
home and made mamma some cabbage-leaf tea,
and she felt better, and I was happy then, just
as we are now."

"Well, maybe that's it," admitted Sammie. "I
am glad Mrs. Wren has a nice home, anyhow.
But I wouldn't like to live away up in a tree,
would you?"

"No, indeed. I would be afraid when the wind
blew and the nest shook."

"It is ever so much nicer underground in our
burrow," continued Sammie.

"It certainly is," agreed Susie, "but I s'pose a
bird, having wings like a plane, would not like
that. They seem to want to be high up in the
air. But I don't like it. Once I hopped away
up on top of Farmer Tooker's woodpile, because
his gray cat chased me, and when I looked down

I was very dizzy, and yet the woodpile was not as high as a tree."

So the two bunny children hurried along, talking of many things, and, now and then, finding some nice sweet roots, or juicy leaves, which they ate. They paused every once in a while to look over the tops of little hills to discover if any dogs or hunters or ferrets were in sight, for the little rabbits did not want to be caught.

At length they came to a little brook that was not far from their home. The edge of the stream had ice on it, for, though Spring was approaching, the weather was still cold.

"Ah! There is some ice. I am going to have a slide!" Sammie shouted.

"You had better not!" cautioned his sister. "You might fall in."

"I will keep close to the shore," promised her brother, and he took a run and slid along the ice. "Come on!" he cried. "It's fun, Susie. Come and slide with me!"

The little bunny girl was just going to walk out on the ice, when Sammie, who had taken an extra long run, slid right off the ice and plop! Into the water he splashed.

"Oh! Oh, Susie!" screamed Sammie. "I've fallen in! Help me out!"

"What shall I do?" cried sister Susie. She

stood up on her hind legs and waved her little paws in the air.

"Get a stick and let me grab it!" called Sammie. "But don't come too close, or you may fall in, too."

Sammie was very fond of his sister, and did not want her to get hurt. He clung to the edge of the ice, and shivered in the cold water, while, with her teeth, Susie gnawed a branch from a tree. The branch she held out to her brother, who grasped it in his mouth and was soon pulled up on shore. But, oh, how he shivered! And how his fur was plastered down all over him, just like a pussy cat when it falls into the bathtub. But I hope none of you children ever put pussy in there.

"You must run home at once," said Susie, "and drink some hot sassafras tea, so you won't take cold. Come on, I'll run with you, Sammie!"

So they started off, running, hopping, leaping and bounding, and, by the time they got to their burrow, Sammie was quite warm. Down the front door hole the little rabbits plunged, and, as soon as Sammie's mother saw him, she cried out:

"Why, Sammie! You've been in swimming! Didn't I tell you never to go in swimming?"

"I haven't been swimming, mother," said Sammie.

"Yes, you have; your hair is all wet," answered Mrs. Littletail suspicious like.

Then Sammie told how he had fallen in through the ice. Uncle Wiggily Longears, the old rabbit, heard him, and said he guessed he would have to give Sammie and Susie some lessons in swimming.

So if the dill pickle will dance with the rye bread in the cottage cheese, I'll tell you next something about Nurse Jane.

STORY X

JANE FUZZY-WUZZY GIVES A LESSON

UNCLE WIGGILY was a very wise old rabbit. He had lived so long, and had escaped so many dogs and hunters, year after year, that he knew about all that any rabbit can know. Of course, that may not be so very much, but it was a good deal for Uncle Wiggily Longears. So, the day after Sammie came home from having fallen in the brook, the old rabbit gentleman got ready to give Sammie and Susie Littletail their swimming lesson.

"You will want to know how to get out of the water when you fall in," he said. "So come with me, and I will show you. It is not very cold out, and I will give you a short lesson."

"Be careful not to let them drown," cautioned Mamma Littletail.

"I will," promised Uncle Wiggily, and he started from the burrow house followed by the two bunny children. But, just as Mr. Longears reached the front door he was seized with a sharp spasm of rheumatism.

"Oh! oh! oh, dear!" he cried three times, just like that.

"What is the matter?" asked Sammie.

"Rheumatism," answered Uncle Wiggily and he put his left front paw on his left hind leg. "I have it very bad. I don't believe I would dare go in the water with you children to-day. We shall have to postpone the swimming lesson. Yet I don't like to, as you ought to learn to swim. I wonder if you could learn if I stood on the bank and told you what to do?"

"I think it would be much better if you could come into the water and show us," said Susie. She was timid about water.

"Yes, of course it would," admitted Uncle Wiggily. "Of course it would, my dear, only you see—ouch! Oh, me! Oh, my!" and poor Uncle Wiggily wrinkled his pink nose and made it twinkle like a star on a frosty night, and he twiddled his ears to and fro. "Oh, that was a terrible sharp pain," he said. "I don't believe I'd better go, my dears. I'm awfully sorry——"

"Let me take the children and show them how to swim," offered Nurse Jane Fuzzy-Wuzzy, who had just finished peeling the potatoes for dinner. She could peel them very nicely with her long, sharp front teeth, which were just like a chisel that a carpenter uses to cut splinters from a board.

"Yes, I guess you could teach them, Nurse Jane," said Uncle Wiggily, as he rubbed his rheumatic leg softly. "You are a much better swimmer than I am; but can you spare the time from the housework?"

Miss Fuzzy-Wuzzy had to do much of the housework for the Littletail family, but, as she was a very good muskrat, she was able to do it, and she often had time to spare, so she answered:

"Yes, I can just as well go as not, for I have the dinner on the stove, and Mrs. Littletail will not be home to lunch. I will give the children a swimming lesson. It will not take long."

"Well," spoke Uncle Wiggily. "I wish you would. I must go to Dr. Possum's and get something for my rheumatism."

"You had better try a hot cabbage leaf," said Miss Fuzzy-Wuzzy. "I have heard that is good for all rabbit aches and pains."

"I will," said the old bunny gentleman, as he crawled back down into the burrow, while Susie and Sammie, with Nurse Jane Fuzzy-Wuzzy, went on to the brook.

The muskrat lady was a very good swimmer, indeed, and as soon as she reached the water she

plunged in and swam about, to show Sammie
and Susie how it ought to be done. She dived,
and she shot across the brook like an aquaplane.
She swam on her side, and in the ordinary style.
In fact, Nurse Jane swam in a number of ways
that you and I could not. At length she swam
entirely under water for some distance, and the
bunny children were afraid she was drowned, but
she came up smiling, showing her sharp teeth,
and explained that this was one of the ways she
used to escape from dogs, boys and other ene-
mies.

Then the muskrat lady gave the bunny children their lesson. She had little trouble in teach-
ing them, as they learned quickly. She was just
showing them how to float along with only the
tip of the nose showing, in order to keep out of
sight, when, suddenly, there was a noise on the
bank.

No, it was not some one after the bunny rabbit
children's clothes, for they had left them at home
when they went to take a lesson and wore only
bathing suits. But it was a number of boys with
a dog, who were making the noise. As soon as
the boys saw the rabbits and Nurse Jane they
picked up a lot of stones, and one boy cried out:

"Oh, look there! Two rabbits and a muskrat!
Let's catch 'em and sell their skins!"

"Oh, dear!" exclaimed Susie, who was very much frightened. "Whatever shall we do?"

"Don't be alarmed," said Nurse Jane Fuzzy-Wuzzy, speaking calmly and formal like, as she started to swim down stream. "Just follow me; swim as I do, with only your nose out of water, and I will save you."

The boys ran along the bank, throwing stones at the bunnies and Nurse Jane, the dog barked.

If the piece of toast doesn't try to play ball with the soft-boiled egg, I'll tell you next about a terrible time.

STORY XI

SAMMIE'S AND SUSIE'S TERRIBLE TIME

YOU may be sure the two Littletail children were very much frightened when they were floating down the stream behind Nurse Jane Fuzzy-Wuzzy, with the boys on the bank throwing stones at them, and the dog barking as hard as he could bark.

"Sick the dog in the water after them," called one boy.

"Naw! This dog doesn't like water," said the boy who owned it. "We'll hit 'em with stones, and then poke 'em out with sticks."

Oh, how Sammie and Susie shuddered when they heard those words! They did not know Miss Fuzzy-Wuzzy was going to save them. The muskrat looked around to see how the children were swimming.

"Don't be afraid," she called, but of course the boys could not understand what she said. The dog could, being an animal and understand-

53

ing animal talk, but the dog couldn't tell the boys
for he couldn't speak boy talk.

"Don't be afraid," said Nurse Jane. "Sammie, keep your head farther under water. Susie,
strike out harder with your forepaws."

The two bunny children did as they were told.
Just then a stone came very close to Miss Fuzzy-
Wuzzy, and she went completely beneath the
water.

"The muskrat's gone!" cried a boy.

"No," said another, "it can swim under water.
But don't bother with the rabbits. They're little,
and their fur isn't much good. Kill the muskrat,
for we can get fifty cents for the skin."

"Oh, how mean boys are!" thought Susie Littletail. "To talk about selling poor Nurse Jane
Fuzzy-Wuzzy's skin! Aren't they terrible!"

The boys now gave all their attention to throwing stones at the muskrat, but she was very wise,
and kept under water as much as possible, so
they could not hit her. They did not throw at
Sammie or Susie. Presently Miss Fuzzy-Wuzzy
swam backward under water and came up near
Sammie. She put her sharp nose close to his ear
and whispered:

"Down stream, a little way, is a burrow where
I used to live. The front door is under water,
but if you and Susie hold your breaths you can

dive down, get in and come up in the dry part. Then you can dig a way out, over in a field, and we can all go home, and escape the boys."

Soon, when they came to the place, the two bunny children took long breaths, and dived down under water. Sammie and Susie took hold of the tail of Miss Fuzzy-Wuzzy to guide them in the dark, and, though it seemed a terrible thing not to breathe under water it was soon over. The three suddenly found themselves in a little underground house, much like the rabbits' own, where they could breathe again.

"Now we are safe!" exclaimed the muskrat lady. "Just dig a back door and you can get out."

So Sammie and Susie dug with their paws, and, soon, they found themselves in a nice field, some distance back from the water. They could see the boys and their dog still watching near the bank to catch them and Miss Fuzzy-Wuzzy, and the boys never knew how the muskrat and the rabbit children escaped.

"My! but that was exciting," said Sammie, when they were on their way home.

"Indeed it was," agreed Susie. "I'm so frightened that I have almost forgotten how to swim."

"It will all come back to you the next time you go in the water," said Nurse Fuzzy-Wuzzy.

"But I must hurry home now, or dinner will be late.

They got to the burrow without anything more happening. Mamma Littletail and Uncle Wiggily were much alarmed when told about the little bunnies' narrow escape.

"Those boys!" shouted the old rabbit gentleman. "If I wasn't laid up with rheumatism, I'd show them!" and he snapped his teeth in quite a savage manner indeed, for a rabbit can get angry at times.

After dinner Mamma Littletail asked Sammie and Susie to go to the cabbage-field store for her, but, as Sammie wanted to stay home and make a whistle out of a carrot, Susie went alone. As she was walking along under a big tree, she heard a noise in the branches, and, looking up, she saw a number of squirrels. One was the squirrel who had given her old nest to Mrs. Wren.

The little gray chaps were running about, seemingly much excited over something. Presently they all scampered down, and Susie saw that they had their mouths full of nuts. They put them on the ground in a little heap, and then the little bunny girl noticed that there was, nearby, an old stump, and it was set just like a table, with dried leaves for plates, and the tops of acorns for cups.

"What is going on here?" Susie asked the squirrel whom she knew.

"I am giving a party in honor of having moved into my new nest," said the squirrel. "Wouldn't you like to come?"

"Yes," said Susie very politely, "I would like very much to."

"Then," said the squirrel, "hop up on the stump, and I will get an extra plate for you." Susie did so. It was the first party she had ever attended, but I can't tell you what happened until the next story.

Then, if the umbrella doesn't pour a pint of water in the rubber boot so the gold fish can go swimming you shall hear about the party.

STORY XII

SUSIE GOES TO A PARTY

UP and down the big oak tree scampered the squirrels, bringing nuts and acorns from hollows and holes where they had been hidden all winter.

"Hi, Bushytail!" cried the squirrel whom Susie knew, speaking to another squirrel who was on the ground at the foot of the stump. "Bring up a big leaf."

"What do you want with a big leaf?" inquired the squirrel who was called Bushytail.

"Susie Littletail is going to stay to the party," replied the squirrel who was giving it. "I want the leaf for a plate for her. She will need a large one."

Up the old stump climbed Bushytail, with the leaf in his mouth, and he put it in a vacant place. The stump was quite large enough for the squirrels and little rabbit girl to move about upon, and still leave room for the table to be set. Susie saw the squirrels placing nut meats on the different plates and putting oak-leaf tea into the acorn cups. Suddenly the squirrel whom Susie knew, and whose name was Mrs. Lightfoot, exclaimed:

"There! I never thought of that!"

"Thought of what?" asked Susie.

"Why, we haven't anything that you like to eat, my dear. You don't care for nuts, do you?"

"Not very much," answered Susie, who wanted to be polite, yet who still wanted to tell the truth.

"I thought so," spoke Mrs. Lightfoot. "Whatever shall I do? I've asked you to the party and now there is nothing you like to eat. It's too bad, for I want you to have a good time."

"I—I could go to the cabbage-field store and get some leaves, and I could also bring some carrots and eat them," suggested Susie.

"Yes, but it wouldn't be right to ask you to a party and then have you bring your own things to eat," objected Mrs. Lightfoot. "That would never do!"

"That's what they do at surprise parties," went on Susie, who had heard Uncle Wiggily tell of a party he once attended. It was given by a chipmunk who wore a striped coat.

"Yes, but this isn't a surprise party," said Mrs. Lightfoot. "I don't know what to do. Dear me!"

"We can pretend it's a surprise party," went

on Susie, politely. "I know I was very much surprised when you asked me to come to it."

"Were you, indeed?" inquired the lady squirrel. "Then a surprise party it shall be. Listen!" she called to the other squirrels; "this is a surprise party for Susie Littletail."

"Humph! I don't call this a surprise," grumbled an old squirrel, whose tail had partly been shot off. But nobody minded him, as he was always grumbling. So Susie scampered away, got some cabbage leaves and carrots, and brought them to the party. She had to eat them all alone, as the squirrels did not care much for such things. The only thing Susie could eat, which the squirrels also ate, was some ice cream, made with snow, maple syrup and hickory nuts ground up fine. This was very good.

Susie had a grand time at the party. After the hickory-nut ice cream and other good things had been eaten, she and the squirrels played "Ring Around the Old Oak Stump," which is something like "London Bridge" and "Ring Around the Rosey" mixed up together. It was lots of fun, and Susie almost forgot to go to the cabbage-field store where her mother had sent her. But she finally reached there, though the store was just about to be closed up. And when Susie got home with the cabbage leaves for sup-

per, she told about the surprise party. Then
Sammie wished he had gone to the store, instead
of remaining at home to make a whistle out of a
carrot.

"I never had anything nice like that happen
to me," said Sammie, in just the least bit of a
grumbly voice. And, what do you think? The
very next day something happened to Sammie,
only it wasn't very nice. He was out walking
in a field, when he met a big cat.

"Where do you live?" asked the cat, in quite
a friendly voice, and sort of confidential like.

"Over there," said Sammie, pointing toward
the burrow.

"Can you take me there?" asked the cat, and
she wiggled her whiskers and licked her nose with
her tongue, for she was hungry. Oh! But she
was a sly cat!

"Yes, I'll show you," agreed Sammie, and he
led the cat toward the burrow.

Now Sammie did not know any better, for he
did not stop to think that cats will eat rabbits.
And the cat was just thinking how easily she had
provided a good dinner for herself, when Miss
Fuzzy-Wuzzy, who was peeping out of the front
door of the burrow, saw pussy.

The muskrat lady knew at once that the cat
had come to eat the little rabbits and the big ones,

too, and the only reason the cat did not eat Sammie was because she wanted more of a meal. So the nurse opened her mouth and showed her sharp teeth, and the cat ran away. But now she knew where the burrow was, and this was a sad thing, for the plotting cat might come back again in the night, when Sammie and Susie were asleep.

"We must move away from here at once," said Uncle Wiggily, when he heard about the cat. "We must find a new burrow or make one. Sammie, you acted very wrongly, but you did not mean to, talking to that cat. Now, you must help us pack up to move."

And next, if all goes well, I shall tell you what happened when the Littletail family went to their new home.

But I hope the gold fish doesn't try to take a shower bath in the fountain pen or it may have to write a letter of apology.

STORY XIII

THE LITTLETAIL FAMILY MOVE

DID you ever see a rabbit family move? No, I
don't suppose you have, for not every one has
had that chance. But the Littletail family, as I
told you in the other story, found they must move
because a big cat had found out where their burrow was.

"I shall go out at once, and see if I can find a
new place," said Uncle Wiggily, after the excite-
ment, caused by Sammie bringing home the cat,
had partly calmed down. "We need a larger
burrow, anyhow. I will find a nice one," said
Mr. Longears.

"Can you go out with your rheumatism?"
asked Mamma Littletail. "You are very lame,
you know, Uncle Wiggily. Perhaps you had
better wait until Papa Littletail comes home to-
night, and he will go."

"No, we must lose no time," said the rabbit
uncle. "I can manage with my crutch, I guess."

So he started out from the burrow, leaning

heavily on a crutch Nurse Jane Fuzzy-Wuzzy had gnawed out of a cornstalk.

"Be careful of the cat," cautioned Susie.

"Oh, no cat can catch me, even if I have the rheumatism very bad," said her uncle, and he limped away. While he was gone, Nurse Jane Fuzzy-Wuzzy promised to keep a sharp lookout for that cat.

Uncle Wiggily Longears was gone for some time. When he returned to the burrow Papa Littletail had come back from where he worked in a carrot factory, which was a new position for him, with social security and all that, and he had heard the news.

"Well," Mr. Littletail asked Uncle Wiggily, "did you find a new burrow?"

"Yes," answered the rabbit uncle, "I did. I will tell you all about it. I hopped a long distance, and I met several friends of mine. I asked them about burrows, and they said the best ones were all taken. I was afraid you would have to dig a new one, until I met Mr. Ground-hog, and he told me of a burrow next to his, on the bank of a little pond. We can get it cheap, he said."

"Has it all improvements?" asked Mamma Littletail. "I want a good kitchen and a bath-room."

"It has everything," said the rabbit uncle. "It has three doors, and we can get in and out easily. It is near a cabbage-field and a turnip patch. We can bathe in the pond, so we won't need a bathroom."

"Where is the burrow?" asked Papa Littletail. "It must be near the trolley, you know."

"It is not far from the cars," went on Uncle Wiggily. "Have you ever heard of Eagle Rock?"

None of the family had.

"Well, it is not far from there," said Uncle Wiggily. "I went out on the rock, and my! What a view there was! I could see away over the big meadows, where some of your relatives live, Miss Fuzzy-Wuzzy, and then I could see a place called New York."

"What's New York?" asked Susie Littletail.

"I don't know," answered her uncle promptly. "I imagine it must be something good to eat."

But of course, children, you know how mistaken he was. New York is a big city. Uncle Wiggily told more about his hop-walk, and finally the rabbit family decided to take the new burrow, so the cat could not find them.

The next day the Littletails moved. That is all they did, they just moved. They had no packing or unpacking to do, except that Sammie

took the whistle he had made out of a carrot and
Uncle Wiggily carried his cornstalk crutch. By
noon they were all settled, and Nurse Jane
Fuzzy-Wuzzy had cooked some of the cabbage,
which had been left in the field all winter, and
also some turnips, which were piled under a lot
of straw out-of-doors. She also found some potatoes, which she peeled with her sharp teeth.

That afternoon, as Sammie was hopping about
his new home, he heard some one exclaim:

"Hello!"

"Hello," replied Sammie, who always wanted
to be friendly.

"Where do you live?" the voice went on, and,
all at once, Sammie thought of the cat.

"No, you don't!" he cried. "You can't fool
me again. I know you!"

"Oh, do you?" asked the voice. "Well, seeing
that I'm a stranger here, and you are, also, I
don't think that you know me."

Sammie looked on top of a clod of earth,
whence the voice came, and saw a big frog.

"Oh, it's you, is it?" he asked faintly but still
not understanding.

"Of course," replied the frog. "My name's
Bully; what's yours?" Sammie told him.

"Ever hear of me?" went on the frog, and
when Sammie said he had not, the frog croak-

ingly continued: "Well, let's see who can jump
the farthest," and with that he began to get
ready. Sammie, who was a very good jumper,
also prepared himself for a hop, and, just as they
were about to see who was the better jumper,
there suddenly— But there, I shall have to wait
until the next story to tell you what happened.

But if the rain coat doesn't stop dribbling
water on the ironing board to dampen the dry
ice, the next story will be about a surprise.

STORY XIV

HOW THE WATER GOT IN

LET me see, where did I leave off last?

Oh, I remember now, I was telling you about Sammie Littletail's new playmate, Bully, the frog, and how they were about to start a jumping contest, when something happened. This is what happened:

Bully was crouching down for a spring, when he suddenly looked up. This was not hard for him, as his eyes were nearly on top of his head, but Sammie had to get on his hind legs to peer upward properly. And this is what both little creatures saw:

A big bird, with long legs and a very long bill, was standing on one leg right over the frog. The bird was looking intently at Bully.

"Come on!" cried the frog to the rabbit. "We must get away from here as quickly as we can."

"Why?" asked Sammie Littletail.

"Because," said Bully, "that bird will eat us. My father warned me never to stay near that bird. Let's go away at once."

"What sort of a bird is it?" asked Sammie, who now had no wish to jump. "I'm sure it can't be very harmful. The only birds that I have to look out for are owls, eagles and hawks, and this bird isn't any of them."

"No, I'm not one of them," spoke the bird with the long legs, snapping its bill as if sharpening it. "I'm a blue heron, that's what I am, though some folks think I'm a stork or a crane."

"Well," spoke Sammie, "you're not dangerous, are you?"

"Not for you," went on the blue heron, and he snapped his beak again, just like scissors. "I came for that fellow," and the bird lowered the leg it had hidden under its feathers and pointed at the frog. "I came for you," the blue heron went on. "You're wanted at once. What's your name?"

Sammie Littletail thought the bird might have asked the frog's name first, before saying that Bully was wanted, but the bird did not seem to consider this.

"What's your name?" the long-legged bird asked again.

"Bully," answered the frog, in a trembling, croaking voice.

"Humph!" exclaimed the heron. "That's a good name. Mine is Billy. Bully and Billy go well together. I'm called Billy because I have such a long bill, you see," the heron explained to Sammie Littletail. "But enough of this. I've come for you, Bully. I'm hungry. I'm going to eat you. That's why you're wanted at once and immediate."

"I—I think there must be some mistake," faltered Bully.

"No mistake at all," snapped the heron. "It's in all the books. Cranes, storks and herons always eat frogs, mice and-so-forth. I never ate any and-so-forth, but I imagine it must be very nice. At any rate, I'm going to eat you!" and he snapped his bill like three knives being sharpened on a whetstone.

"Oh, are you?" cried Bully, the frog, and he suddenly gave a great jump, greater even than that which the Jumping Frog, that Mark Twain wrote about gave, and into the pond Bully plunged, and went right to the bottom. Now, what do you think about that? Yes, sir, Bully went right to the bottom, where the blue heron couldn't get him, and then Bully called up, in a voice which sounded very hoarse because it came from so far under water:

"Ha! Ha! Who got left?"

"I suppose he means me," spoke the heron to Sammie, and the bird, very much annoyed,

fanned itself with its long leg. "I don't believe
that's fair," the heron went on. "It's in all the
books that I should eat frogs." Then, with a
great flapping of wings, the tall creature flew
away, and Bully, the frog, came out of the water.

"You had a narrow escape," said Sammie.

"Oh, I'm used to that," replied the frog.
"Now, let's practice jumping."

Which they did, only the frog always jumped
into the water and Sammie remained on dry
land, so they never could tell who was the best at
it. Then they played other games, and became
very good friends. The frog pond was very near
the new burrow where Sammie lived, and the
two friends used to meet quite often. One day
the frog said:

"I think it would be very nice if you would dig
a way from your burrow to my pond. Then,
when it rained, I could come to see you without
getting wet, and you could come to see me."

"That is a fine idea," declared Sammie. "I'll
do it."

So, without saying anything to his mother or
sister or Uncle Wiggily, little rabbit Sammie began to dig under-ground to reach the pond. It
took him some time, but at last he came out of a
hole just above the top of the water, near where
Bully lived.

"This is great!" cried the frog, as he looked in the hole. "Now when it rains we will not get wet. Fine work, Sammie!"

And, what do you think? It rained that very night. It rained so hard that the pond rose higher and higher, until the water began to run in the hole that Sammie had dug. The noise of the water awakened the Littletail family in the middle of the night, and when Uncle Wiggily saw the water creeping nearer and nearer to him, and felt the rheumatism worse than ever, he cried out:

"A flood! A flood! We must swim out, or we shall all be drowned."

Now in the next story you shall hear what took place. But please ask the big hand to stop chasing the little hand of the clock until it has time to wash its face.

STORY XV

SAMMIE AND SUSIE AT THE CIRCUS

OF course, you remember how Sammie Littletail dug a tunnel from the burrow to the pond,
and how the water came in. Of course. Well,
Nurse Jane Fuzzy-Wuzzy made a raft of corn-
stalks, and on this the whole rabbit family floated
out of the burrow. Bully, the frog, who was a
playmate of Sammie's, helped them. They had
to go right out into the rain, and it was not very
pleasant.

"Whatever are we going to do?" asked Mamma Littletail. But she did not scold Sammie for
digging the tunnel and making all the trouble.
She was a kind rabbit mother, wasn't she?

"We must get in out of the wet, or my rheumatism will be so bad I shall not be able to walk,"
complained Uncle Wiggily Longears.

"I know what we can do," proposed the muskrat nurse.

"What?" asked Susie Littletail.

"We can ask Mr. Groundhog to let us stay all

73

night in his burrow," suggested Nurse Jane. "I'm sure he will let us, for he has plenty of room."

Mr. Groundhog, who was an elderly woodchuck gentleman, very fond of sleep in the winter, welcomed the rabbits to his burrow, and there they stayed out of the rain. In the morning the sun was shining brightly, and, before very long, the water all dried out of the bunnies' house, so that they could go back in it.

One day, about a week after this, when Uncle Wiggily was out walking with Sammie and Susie, going quite slowly, because he was a trifle lame from rheumatism, Bully, the frog, came hopping up to them.

"Are you going to the circus?" he asked.

"Circus? What circus?" asked Sammie, who was interested very quickly, you may be sure.

"Why, the animal circus that is always held in the woods every spring. They do all sorts of queer things to get ready for the summer. I'm going. It's lots of fun. Better come," croaked Bully the frog.

"I haven't seen any circus posters up," remarked Susie.

"Of course not," answered Bully. "The animals never put them up, because they don't want a lot of people coming to look on and bother

them. Don't you want to come? It isn't very
far from here."

"But we have no one to take us," spoke Susie.

"Yes, you have!" exclaimed Uncle Wiggily
quickly. "I will take you myself. It would
never do for you children to go to a circus alone."

"But your rheumatism is so bad you can
hardly walk," objected Susie. "Besides, it will
be worse if you sit in the woods."

"Never mind about that," answered the rabbit
uncle bravely. "I'll manage to stand it. I am
determined you children shall not go to that
circus alone. Of course, I don't care anything
about a circus myself, but I must take care of
you," and the elderly rabbit gentleman looked
very brave, though the pain of his rheumatism
was quite bad.

"My father in the circus is going to hop over
three stumps," said Bully, the frog, quite
proudly. "Come on, or we may be late."

So Uncle Wiggily took Sammie and Susie to
the animal circus, and Bully, the frog, went also.
He had a free ticket, because his father was one
of the performers. They had reserved seats on
big toadstools, though Bully said they ought to
be called frogstools, as frogs used them more
than toads did.

Then the performance began, after the birds

had sung an opening chorus. The bunny children had a jolly time. They saw some pigeons give airship exhibitions that were better than any flying machines you ever heard of. They watched the snakes make hoops of themselves, through which, jumped squirrels and rabbits. It was so exciting that Uncle Wiggily clapped his paws as hard as he could. Then Dr. Possum, who was not very busy taking care of sick people that day, hung downward from a limb by his tail ever so long.

When Bully's papa jumped over three big stumps at once, without so much as touching one—well, you should have heard the clapping and shouting then! Best of all, Sammie and Susie liked the baby deer, who stood up on his hind legs and danced, while a crow whistled.

It was so exciting that Sammie and Susie almost forgot to eat the candy-covered carrots and the molasses-cabbage fudge which their uncle bought for them. It was the best time they had ever remembered, and they talked of nothing else on their way home. Even Uncle Wiggily's rheumatism seemed better. Now, if the postage stamp doesn't hop off the envelope and stick on the sidewalk, I am going to tell you next of an adventure Sammie Littletail had with a snake.

STORY XVI

SAMMIE AND THE SNAKE

"SAMMIE," said Mamma Littletail to her little bunny boy one fine day, "I wish you would take this basket of cabbage leaves and preserved clover over to Mr. Groundhog. He was so good to let us stay in his burrow that night the flood came in here that I want to do him a kindness."

"Can't Susie come, too, mamma?" asked Sammie, who did not like to go through the woods alone, especially since there were so many boys wandering about on top of the Orange Mountain, now that Spring was here.

"Yes, Susie may go if she wants to," answered the rabbit childrens' mother. "Do you want to, dear?"

"Oh, yes. I'll go with Sammie. But I think he ought to carry the basket," said Susie.

"Of course I will," said Sammie, so the two bunnies hopped to the burrow where Mr. Groundhog had his home. It was not far from the underground house where the rabbit family lived, and the animal children soon reached it. They knocked on the door, and a voice called out:

"Who's there?"

"Sammie and Susie Littletail," answered Sammie. "We have some cabbage leaves and preserved clover that mamma sent you."

"That is very nice," remarked the gentleman groundhog. "Come right in. I am afraid to open the door, you know."

Sammie and Susie walked in and gave Mr. Groundhog the things in the basket.

Then Susie, who was very curious, asked him a question.

"Why didn't you want to come to the door?" she inquired.

"Because," whispered the groundhog, looking around as if afraid some one would see him, "I might see my shadow again, you know, and that would make Winter longer than ever. You know I went out Candlemas Day and I saw my shadow, and it frightened me so I rushed back in here, and I'm not going out again until March 21, which will be just six weeks from now. If I hadn't seen my shadow, Winter would not last so long—at least, that's what people say. I don't know whether to believe them or not. But I am not going out again until warm weather is here,

so I am very glad your mamma sent me something to eat."

The groundhog gave the bunny children some
bits of dried sweet potato he had put away in his
pantry, and they started for home.

"I don't believe much in that shadow business,"
said Sammie, as he and his sister walked along.
"How could a groundhog, seeing his shadow,
make Winter any longer?"

"I don't know," answered Susie, "but it must
be so, because every one says so; even Uncle
Wiggily."

"I'm going to ask Nurse Jane Fuzzy-Wuzzy
when I get home," declared Sammie. "Come on,
let's go 'round by Farmer Tooker's cabbage
patch. Maybe we can find a stump or two to
gnaw. I'm getting hungry. Mr. Groundhog
didn't give me enough sweet potato."

"Perhaps that was all he had," suggested
Susie.

They were walking along, through a little
wood, when, all of a sudden, the two bunnies
heard a hiss, just like the steam coming out of
the radiator.

"What's that?" cried Sammie.

"It's a snake!" shouted Susie. "Look out,
Sammie, or he will grab you."

Sammie tried to jump out of the way, but he was too late, and the big black snake grabbed him. The snake coiled around poor Sammie, and bit the little rabbit's ear to make him keep quiet, I suppose, for Sammie was trying to get loose.

"Oh, oh, oh!" exclaimed Susie. "You bad snake! Let my little brother alone."

But the black snake never said a word, only he clung the tighter to poor Sammie.

"Run for help, Susie!" called the little boy rabbit. "Run and ask Mr. Groundhog to come and drive the snake away!"

So Susie ran as fast as she could, and did not even stop to rap on the burrow door where Mr. Groundhog lived. She went right in, and told the elderly woodchuck gentleman that a bad snake had caught her little brother.

"And won't you please come and get him loose?" asked Susie, who was crying. "If you shut your eyes you won't see your shadow, and be frightened. I will lead you to him."

"Never mind about my shadow!" bravely exclaimed Mr. Groundhog. "I don't care whether I see it again or not. I'll go and save Sammie Littletail, who was so kind to me."

So the woodchuck ran and hit the snake with a club, until the bad chap was glad enough to let Sammie loose, and it was quite time, too, for poor

Sammie's breath was nearly squeezed out of him. Then Sammie, after he had thanked Mr. Groundhog, ran home with Susie.

Now if the roller skate will please stop trying to jump out of the doll's carriage I shall try to tell you next something about Susie and the white kitty.

STORY XVII

SUSIE AND THE WHITE KITTY

SUSIE LITTLETAIL had gone for a walk in the woods. It was Spring, but the little bunny girl did not go to see if there were any wildflowers peeping up. Indeed, she cared very little about flowers, except the kind that were good to eat, and these were mostly clover blossoms. So that is what Susie went out to look for.

Uncle Wiggily Longears had said to her that day: "It seems to me, Susie, that it's getting quite warm out. My rheumatism is better, and it never does get better unless it's getting warm. So, of course, it must be getting warm."

Susie thought so, too.

"Then if it's getting warmer it must really be Spring," went on her uncle. "Now, if I were you, I would go take a walk and see how the clover is coming on. Some nice, fresh clover would taste very good."

"I'll see if I can get you any," spoke Susie,

who was a very good little rabbit girl, and who always was kind to her old uncle.

So that is why she was walking in the woods. She was almost through the place where the tall trees grew, and was just going to step out into a field, that looked as if it had clover in it, when she heard a funny little noise. It was a sort of a squeak, and at first Susie thought it might be Nurse Jane Fuzzy-Wuzzy, for, sometimes, the muskrat lady housekeeper started off with a squeak when she wanted to talk. But it was not her nurse whom Susie saw. Instead it was a dear little pussy kitten.

"Did you make that funny noise?" asked the little rabbit girl of the kitten.

"Yes," answered pussy, "but I don't call it a funny noise."

"I do," went on Susie.

"It was not at all funny, and I don't see anything to laugh at," spoke pussy, and then Susie saw that the white kitten had a large tear in each eye. "That was a mew," the kitty said.

"Why did you mew, pussy?" asked Susie.

"Because I am lost, and I don't know my way home. I guess you would mew if you couldn't find your papa or mamma."

"No," said Susie, "I wouldn't mew, but I

would be very much frightened. But why don't you go home?" Susie sat up and wrinkled her nose, just like water when it bubbles in the tea kettle, for that was the way Susie used her nose to smell, and she wanted to see if she could smell danger.

"How can I go home when I don't know the way?" asked the white kitten.

"Which way did you come in here?" said Susie.

"If I knew that, I would know which way to go back home," the pussy replied, and the large tears, one in each eye, fell out and dropped on the ground, while two more tears came into her eyes.

"Are you crying because you are lost?" asked Susie.

"Of course. Wouldn't you?"

"Perhaps," answered Susie. "But you see I never was lost. I can always smell my way home, no matter how far off I go," and Susie wiggled her nose so fast that it made the kitty quite cross-eyed to watch it, and being cross-eyed made pussy sneeze. Then pussy felt better after her sneeze.

"Can you show me the way home?" asked the kitty of Susie, hopeful like.

"Not to your house, for I don't know where it

is," answered Susie, "but I could show you the way to mine."

Then the white kitty wanted Susie to do this, but the little rabbit girl thought it might not be safe, for the little kittie might show the big cats where the new underground house was.

"What is your name?" asked Susie of the kittie.

"My name is Ann Gora, but every one calls me Ann."

"That is a funny name," said Susie.

"I don't think it is at all," went on the kitten. "It is no funnier than Susie," and the pussy began to cry again.

"Oh, don't cry!" exclaimed Susie kindly, and she patted the kitty on the back with her paw. "Come with me. We will walk through the field, and maybe we will see your house. I think you must live in a house with people, for kitties never live in the woods like the squirrels, or in burrows as we do. We will look until we find a house with people in it, and maybe you belong there," said Susie.

"That will be fine!" mewed the kittie, and she dried her tears on her paw.

So Susie and the kitty walked on together. And pretty soon Susie saw a little girl coming toward them. The little girl was looking in the grass, and calling, "Ann—Ann," in a soft voice. And when she saw the little kitty she ran to her and caught her up in her arms and hugged her.

Then Susie Littletail ran home, for she was afraid of little girls, and on the way Susie saw that the clover was coming up nicely, so she told Uncle Wiggily.

Now, if it is not too cold to-morrow and the door knob doesn't turn over in its sleep, I am going to tell you about Sammie and the black doggie.

STORY XVIII

SAMMIE AND THE BLACK DOGGIE

ONE day, when Sammie Littletail was on his way home from Dr. Possum's house, where he had gone to get some sweet-flag root, for Uncle Wiggily Longears' rheumatism, something happened to the little boy rabbit. He was coming through a big field, where the grass was quite high, when he heard a little bark. He knew at once that it was a dog, and Sammie was afraid of dogs, as all rabbits are, so he started to run. But the dog called out:

"Don't run, little rabbit."

"Why not?" asked Sammie. "I'm afraid of you."

"But I won't hurt you," went on the dog.

"You might," answered Sammie. "Dogs always hurt rabbits."

"Not all dogs," continued the little black one. "Besides, I am what they call a doggie. A dog-

gie is a small dog, you know, and small dogs
won't hurt rabbits."

"Are you sure?" asked Sammie.

"Perfectly sure. Besides, I am a trick dog,
and trick dogs are so well fed at home that they
do not have to hunt rabbits to eat."

"Are you sure?" asked Sammie again.

"Perfectly sure. You just watch me, and you
will see that I do not eat you. Watch me carefully."

"Oh, I meant are you sure that you are a trick
dog," went on Sammie.

"Of course, I am sure. I can do lots of tricks.
I can play dead. I can turn a back somersault,
and I can walk on my hind legs——"

"Oh, I can do that, too," interrupted Sammie.

"Yes, I know. I saw you do that a little
while ago. But can you walk on your front legs,
with your hind legs up in the air? Now, can you
do that?" and the black doggie looked straight
at Sammie.

"I never tried that," replied Sammie.

"No; and I guess you'd better not, unless you
want to fall. I fell lots of times before I learned
it. But I can do it now, and every time I do my
master gives me a sweet cracker," said the black
doggie.

"What's a sweet cracker?" asked Sammie, who thought it sounded very nice.

"Don't you know what a sweet cracker is?" asked the doggie, who was much surprised.

"No, I don't," declared Sammie.

"Well, you ought to. I'm astonished at you. It's sweet, and it's a cracker, that's all I can tell you. You ought to know such things yourself."

"Look here!" said Sammie, who thought the doggie was trying to show how smart he was, "do you know what molasses carrots are?"

"No," answered the doggie. "I don't believe there are any such things."

"Yes, there are," declared Sammie politely. "I have had them to eat. So, you see, if I don't know what a sweet cracker is, you don't know what molasses carrots are. We're even now."

"Oh, let's talk about something else," said the doggie quickly. "I will show you some of my tricks, if you would like to see them."

"I would like to see them very much," answered Sammie, more politely than before.

So the little black doggie walked on his hind legs, and then he walked on his front legs. Next, he played dead, and Sammie was quite frightened, until, with a bark, the doggie jumped up and turned three back somersaults, one after the

other, just as easy as you can upset the salt-
cellar. After that he rolled over and sneezed like
any boy or girl, it was so natural.

Sammie was becoming very much interested,
for the doggie's tricks were almost as good as
those Sammie had seen at the circus, when, all
at once, who should come along but a big man.
He whistled to the little black doggie, and the
doggie, who was trying to stand on the end of his
tail, got down and ran to the man. Sammie was
so frightened that he ran, too, only he ran home.

Sammie told his papa and mamma and Susie
and Uncle Wiggily what had happened to him,
and they told him he must be careful not to go
near black doggies again.

"Oh," promised Sammie, "I won't, you may be
sure. But, Uncle Wiggily, are squirrels all
right to play with?"

"Oh, yes, squirrels are very nice," said his
Uncle. "Why, did you see some?"

"Yes, I met two, and they said their names
were Billie and Johnnie Bushytail, and they are
coming over to see me some time."

"That will be nice," remarked Susie. "May I
play with them, too?"

"I guess so," replied Sammie. "But, mamma,
I'm hungry. Isn't there anything to eat?"

"You can have some bread and butter," said his mamma.

"With sugar on?" asked Sammie.

"We are all out of sugar," went on Mrs. Littletail. "You must hop to the store for some."

"I will," promised Sammie, "after I eat something."

"All out of sugar," remarked Uncle Wiggily. "That reminds me, I must make some maple sugar soon. I will have it when Billie and Johnnie Bushytail come over to see you; or, perhaps before then, if you are good children."

Sammie and Susie said they would be good, and in another book after this one, I'm going to tell you about Billie and Johnnie Bushytail, the little boy squirrels, and what they did. They lived near Sammie and Susie Littletail. But the next story will be about Uncle Wiggily making maple sugar; that is if the gas stove doesn't bake the jelly-beans so brown that they look like molasses candy.

STORY XIX

UNCLE WIGGILY MAKES MAPLE SUGAR

UNCLE WIGGILY LONGEARS hopped out of the burrow. First he stretched one leg, then he stretched another leg; then he gave a big, long stretch to his third leg, and then he stretched his fourth leg. Next he wiggled both ears, one after the other, and said:

"I feel very fine indeed! Oh, yes, and a boiled carrot besides; very fine!" He looked up at the blue sky, which had some little white clouds on it, just like small snowbanks, or bits of lamb's wool. "I never knew when I felt better," went on Uncle Wiggily. "Even my rheumatism does not hurt much." Just then he saw Nurse Jane Fuzzy-Wuzzy coming out of the burrow, and he spoke to her: "Aren't Sammie and Susie up yet?" he asked.

"They are just washing their faces and paws, getting ready for breakfast," answered the muskrat nurse. "They will soon be out."

92

Sure enough, in a little while the two bunny children came running out.

"Oh, what a lovely day!" laughed Susie Little-tail, and she wrinkled up her nose, and made it go very fast, almost as fast as an automobile or a motorcycle. "Doesn't to-day smell fine?" she asked her brother, and she took a good, long breath.

"It smells just like Spring," answered Sammie. "The wind is nice and warm, there are lots more birds around than there were, and the grass is getting greener and greener every minute." Sammie turned a somersault, he felt so glad that Summer was coming soon.

"Ha! Ha! Ha!" exclaimed Uncle Wiggily, three times, just like that. "Now I know what makes me feel so fine. It is because Spring is here. We must get ready to make maple sugar."

"What is maple sugar?" asked Susie.

"What? I am surprised at you, Susie!" exclaimed Sammie. "Maple sugar is that brown, sweet stuff you buy in the store, and in the Winter you eat it on your pancakes, or you can shave it up and put it on hot rice, or you can put it on fritters. That is what maple sugar is."

"Exactly," went on Uncle Wiggily, and he stretched the leg with the rheumatism in so that it hardly hurt him a bit. "Well, children, we are going to make some maple sugar. Come with me, and I will show you how. Nurse Jane Fuzzy-Wuzzy, we shall have to ask you to help us. We need your sharp teeth to gnaw a hole in the tree."

So Uncle Wiggily, Sammie, Susie and Nurse Jane Fuzzy-Wuzzy went off into the woods. Oh, it was a beautiful day, and in some places the tiny green leaves on the trees were just beginning to show through the brown buds.

"Just think," said Uncle Wiggily, as they walked along. "It will soon be Easter. And, oh! what a lot of work we rabbits will have then, with all the eggs to look after. For, you see, rabbits always have to take charge of the Easter eggs, but of course you know that."

So the rabbits and the muskrat nurse kept on through the woods, leaving Papa and Mamma Littletail at home in the burrow.

Uncle Wiggily walked on ahead, and pretty soon he came to a tree, where he stopped.

"This is a maple tree," he said, "and we can get some juice from it to make maple sugar, so as to have it ready for Easter. Miss Jane Fuzzy-Wuzzy, will you kindly bite a hole in that tree?"

"Of course I will," answered the muskrat lady. She stood up on her hind legs, and gnawed a little hole in the tree. Then Uncle Wiggily took a stem of last year's goldenrod, that was hollow, and put it in the hole. Pretty soon, what should happen but that some juice, like water, began running out of that tree right through the hollow stem of the golden rod.

"That is maple sap," said the old rabbit gentleman, "and when we boil it we shall have maple sugar. Susie, you get an old tin can to catch the sap in, and Sammie, you build a fire to boil it over."

So Susie got an old tomato can, and put it under the place where the juice was running out, and pretty soon, not so very long, the can was full. By that time Sammie and Nurse Jane Fuzzy-Wuzzy had a fire built. Then they hung the can of sap over the fire, and it boiled, and it boiled, and it boiled. It took quite some time, but Uncle Wiggily tried it every now and then by pouring a little of the hot syrup on some snow he found in a hollow place.

"Eat this," he said to Susie and Sammie, when it was cool; and, oh, maybe it wasn't good! Better than the best candy you ever tasted! Then they boiled the sap and boiled it some more, and pretty soon, just as true as I'm telling you, that sap turned into maple sugar. Now, what do you think about that, eh? Well, maybe those bunny

---

rabbit children weren't glad. They made quite a lot of maple sugar, and took some home to Mamma and Papa Littletail, who were very glad to get it. They ate several pieces, and then put some away for Dr. Possum, and his little boy, Possum Pinktoes.

Then Papa Littletail said: "I have just received a letter from some children, who are anxious about their Easter eggs, as it is nearly Easter, so I think we had better begin to get them ready." Uncle Wiggily thought so, too.

Next, if the gum drop doesn't fall down stairs and break the lollypop's stick, I'll tell you about Sammie and the eggs.

STORY XX

SAMMIE AND SUSIE HUNT EGGS

SAMMIE and Susie Littletail were leaping over
the brown leaves and the pine needles in the
woods. There was a little wind blowing, and it
ruffled up the fur on the backs of the rabbit children, but they did not mind that.

"I wonder where we shall find the eggs?"
asked Susie of her brother, and she nibbled a bit
of maple sugar that Uncle Wiggily Longears
had made for them.

"I'm sure I don't know," answered Sammie,
and he, also, ate some of the sweet stuff. "But
we are sure to find them, because Uncle Wiggily
said so. He would have come to show us, only
his rheumatism is worse again."

"We must ask somebody," said Susie, and
just then whom should they see coming along
through the woods but Bully, the frog.

"Hello!" croaked Bully, "let's see who can
jump the farthest, Sammie."

"No," answered the little boy rabbit, "I can't;

97

I am after Easter eggs. Do you know where there are any?"

"Do you mean frogs' eggs?" asked Bully, and he croaked a couple of times, just to keep from getting hoarse.

"I hardly think frogs' eggs would do," and Sammie looked at his sister, and his sister looked at him, until, strange as it may seem, they were both looking at each other.

"No," said Susie, "frogs' eggs would never do. They are not large enough. We must get hens' eggs or ducks' eggs."

"I know where there is a nice duck," went on Bully. "She lives near my pond. Come, and I will take you to her. Maybe she will give you some eggs."

So they all went to where the duck lived. Bully, the frog, hopping ahead, and Sammie and Susie hopping after him, and every time the frog came to a bit of water he hopped in and got all wet, and he didn't mind it a bit, but I'm sure I would. However, pretty soon, they came to where the duck lived.

"Hello, Mrs. Wibblewobble," said Bully to her, for that was the duck's name. Really, it was, I'm not joking. "Mrs. Wibblewobble, here are Sammie and Susie Littletail looking for eggs," said Bully. "Could you let them have any?"

"Quack! quack!" answered the duck, and it sounded just as if she said, "What? What?" So Sammie, thinking she was a little deaf, asked her himself.

"Can you please tell us where we can find some eggs?" and he spoke quite loudly.

"Tut, tut!" exclaimed Mrs. Wibblewobble. "I heard Bully when he asked me the first time. I merely said, 'Quack! quack!' because I was thinking. I always say that when I think. Now be patient." So Mrs. Wibblewobble said "Quack! quack!" again, several times, and paddled around in the water, putting her head under every now and then to dig in the mud for some snails. "No," she finally said, "I have thought very hard, and I do not know where you could find any eggs."

Sammie and Susie were quite disappointed, and Bully said: "Perhaps you have some of your own eggs you could let them have."

"No," answered Mrs. Wibblewobble, "all my eggs have been turned into little ducklings. Here they come now."

Then all at once, as quick as you can scratch your chin, whom should come walking down the pond but the dearest, nicest little ducklings you ever saw. They all said, "Quack! quack!" which, as you know, meant that they were thinking, and

Sammie and Susie, being polite, did not want to disturb them.

"This is my family," proudly announced Mrs. Wibblewobble. "Family, those are the Littletail rabbit children, and Bully, the frog." Then the ducklings all said, "Quack! quack!" again, which this time showed that they had stopped thinking, and they swam around just like their mother.

"Well," said Bully, "we shall get no eggs here. Come on. We will go see Mrs. Cluck-Cluck, the hen. Maybe she has some eggs to spare."

But on their way they lost the road, and didn't know in which direction to go. Then Sammie, Susie and Bully walked on and on until suddenly, they heard a noise in the leaves, oh, such a queer, quiet little noise! Then, what do you think? Why, the sly, sly old fox stuck his head out!

"Whom are you looking for?" he asked, as softly as can be.

"We are looking for Mrs. Cluck-Cluck, to get some eggs," said Sammie.

"Ah, ha! Ho! ho!" laughed the sly old fox. "Come with me and I'll show you her house. I'm sure she has some eggs."

Sammie and Susie thought this very kind of

him, and they were just going to follow the fox
when Bully warned them.

"Don't go," he said; "that fox only wants to
eat Mrs. Cluck-Cluck. Let's run away."

So they ran away, and my! how angry that
fox was, but he couldn't help himself. Then
the three friends walked on and on, until they
were quite tired. They were afraid they would
never find any eggs, when, all of a sudden, they
came right to the place where Mrs. Cluck-Cluck
lived. And, what do you think? She gave Sammie and Susie all the eggs they wanted, and
they carried a great many to the burrow.

Do you think you would like to hear, next,
how Susie learned to jump rope? You see, she
learned while waiting for the time to come to
color Easter eggs.

Well, that story can be told if the egg beater
doesn't punch all the gold fish off the Christmas
tree before they have had their swim.

STORY XXI

SUSIE LITTLETAIL JUMPS ROPE

SAMMIE and Susie Littletail were coming home from school. Didn't I mention before that the little bunny children went to school? Well, I meant to, I'm sure, and if I overlooked it I hope you will excuse me, and I'll see that it does not happen again this Spring or Summer. Oh, my, yes; Sammie and Susie went to school in an old hollow tree, and a mouse was the school teacher— a good, kind Lady Mouse, who never kept the bunny children in.

So, as I said, they were coming home from school, and Sammie had stopped to play marbles with some of his little boy rabbit friends, while Susie walked on with some little rabbit girls. Some of the girls were jumping rope, and they invited Susie to join them.

"Come on," said one little rabbit with two pink eyes, "we will turn for you, and you can have 'three slow, pepper,' Susie dear."

But Susie couldn't, because she didn't know how to jump rope. Now isn't that strange? No, she didn't know the first thing about jumping rope, for she had never had a chance to learn.

So when Susie got home to the burrow that afternoon, and Nurse Jane Fuzzy-Wuzzy had given her a bit of chocolate-covered carrot, Uncle Wiggily Longears noticed that the little rabbit girl looked rather sad.

"What is the matter, Susie?" he asked.

"I can't jump rope," she answered, "and all the other rabbit girls can."

"Never mind," said Uncle Wiggily, "I will show you how. Come with me. Oh, dear! Oh, my goodness me, and some sassafras root! Oh! oh!"

"What is the matter?" asked Susie, much frightened, for she had never heard her uncle cry so loudly before.

"Oh, it's only my rheumatism, Susie dear," he answered. "Don't mind me. I shall be all right presently. Just ask Nurse Jane Fuzzy-Wuzzy to bring me the watercress liniment."

When the muskrat nurse had brought the liniment, and Uncle Wiggily had rubbed some on his leg, he felt better.

"Now, Susie," he said, "I will show you how to jump rope. I used to do it when I was a boy rabbit, but I am not so lively and nimble now as I was then."

"But I have no rope," objected Susie, though she felt a little more happy about what was going to happen. "I can't jump without a rope."

"Tut! tut! Do not think about such a little thing as that," went on her uncle. "I will have a rope for you in a very few minutes. Come with me."

Just then Sammie came along, and, after he had eaten some corn bread with preserved sweet cabbage leaves on it, he went with his sister and uncle in the woods.

"I am going to learn to jump rope," said Susie, quite proudly. "Don't you want to learn, Sammie?"

"No," he said, "that's only for girls. I'd rather play marbles and fly a kite, but I'll turn for you, if we can find a rope," for, you see, Sammie was always kind to his sister.

"We will have a rope in a minute," remarked Uncle Wiggily. "I know where to find it."

Just then who should come walking along but Possum Pinktoes, and, as soon as he saw the rabbits, he pretended to go to sleep.

"Oh, you do not need to go to sleep, and make believe that you are dead," spoke Sammie. "We would not hurt you for the world."

Then Possum Pinktoes, who was only pretending to sleep, as he always did when he thought he was in danger, opened first one eye, then the other.

"I am going to learn to jump rope," said Susie to him.

"Ha! Jump rope, eh? exclaimed Possum Pinktoes. "I know the very thing for you. A wild grapevine! It will make a fine rope."

"That's just what I was going to say," called out Uncle Wiggily.

"Come with me, and I'll show you where there are plenty of vines," went on the little possum boy, so they followed him, and pretty soon they came to the place where the grapevine grew. Sammie and Uncle Wiggily cut a long piece, and then they took hold of each end and began to turn the rope for Susie. At first she could not jump very well, even though there was a nice, smooth, grassy place to learn on. Then out of a pond popped Bully, the frog, and, as he was one of the best jumpers in the woods, or, for that matter, on Orange Mountain, he showed Susie just how to do it.

So she learned to jump "salt," which is slow, and "pepper," which is fast, and "double pepper," which is very fast indeed. Then she learned to jump with two ropes, one going one way and one the other, and finally she could skip as well as any little rabbit girl in the Lady Mouse Teach-

er's Hollow Tree School.   Uncle Wiggily tried
to jump, but he was so stiff and his rheumatism
hurt him so that he couldn't do it very well.

Then they all started for home, and what do
you think happened?   Something quite serious,
I do assure you, and I'm not fooling.   A big
hawk, not the kind, good fish-hawk, but another
kind, who was out looking for early Spring
chickens, swooped down and tried to carry Susie
Littletail off to his nest.

Now Uncle Wiggily was so old he couldn't
do much, but Sammie was not going to see his
little sister harmed, so what did he do but jump
at that hawk with his sharp little feet, and kick
him until the bad bird let go of poor Susie.   She
was quite frightened, but not much hurt, and
she hugged and kissed Sammie for saving her.
Then they all hurried home to the burrow, and
the next story will be about Sammie turning sky-
blue-pink.

But I wish you would ask the piece of cheese
not to jump over the apple pie until it is
sprinkled with sugar.

STORY XXII

SAMMIE COLORED SKY-BLUE-PINK

SUSIE LITTLETAIL was out on a green, grassy place in front of the underground house, jumping her grapevine rope, and having a very good time, indeed. She had gotten all over the fright caused by the bad hawk trying to grab her, and felt quite happy.

Sammie Littletail had been searching for the hawk, to have him arrested for being so cruel to his little rabbit sister, but Sammie could not find the big bird, so he had come back to watch Susie jump. You see it was Easter week, and there was no school. The Lady Mouse Teacher of the Hollow Tree School was very glad of it, too, for she had more time to sleep and doze in the sun.

As Sammie watched Susie finish doing her "three slow, pepper rope jumping," Nurse Jane Fuzzy-Wuzzy came to the door of the burrow and called:

"Sammie, your mamma wants you."

"What does she want?" he asked politely.

"She wants you to go to the drug store and get some dye to color the Easter eggs with. Hurry, please, because she has lots to do," said Nurse Jane.

"May we help color them?" asked Susie, hanging up her grapevine rope on a low bush.

"I think so," answered the muskrat nurse. "Now, hurry, Sammie; your mamma wants to get all the eggs colored before your papa comes home from the carrot factory to-night."

"All right," answered the little boy rabbit. "I guess I can help color the eggs, too," and he hurried off to the drug store, that was near Dr. Possum's house.

Now pretty soon—in fact, almost immediately —something is going to happen to Sammie Littletail, so I want you all to sit quietly, and not wiggle so that you'll make the couch squeak, or I can't go on. That's better.

Well, then, Sammie went through the woods, and, on his way, he felt so happy that he sang this little song, which he had heard the kindergarten children singing at the Hollow Tree School a few days before. This is the song, but of course I can't sing it very well. Please don't laugh. I'll do the best I can, although, perhaps, I shan't get the words just right:

" 'Soldier boy, soldier boy, where are you going,
    Waving so proudly your red, white and
        blue?'
'I'm going to the war to fight for my country,
    And if you'll be a soldier boy, you may come
        too.' "

That's the way Sammie sang it, anyhow, and
just as he finished he reached the drug store.

"Who was that singing?" asked Dr. Possum,
who happened to be in the store just then.

"I was," said Sammie.

"Oh, indeed; I didn't know you sang," went
on Dr. Possum. "That is very good indeed. I
could not do better myself. Will you kindly
sing it again?" So Sammie sang it again, and
then he got the colors for his mamma to put on
the Easter eggs.

"Now, children," said Mamma Littletail,
when Sammie reached home, "get the eggs that
Mrs. Cluck-Cluck gave you the other day, and
we will color them."

"Oh, won't we have fun!" cried Susie.

"Indeed we will!" said Sammie.

So they first boiled the eggs good and hard,
so that if they happened to drop one it wouldn't
splash and plop over the floor. You know how
unpleasant it is, to say the least, when an egg

drops, and skidoodles over the floor. Isn't it, really? Well, they boiled the eggs hard, and then Mamma Littletail made the dye ready.

Well, you should have seen all the colors she had! There was red and blue and yellow and green and purple and pink and old rose and crushed strawberry and ashes of roses and magenta and Alice blue and Johnnie red and Froggie green and toadstool brown and skilligimink. That last, the druggist told Sammie, was a new color, and very scarce. As there isn't any more of it at the drug store, I can't just tell you what it looked like, except that it was a very fine color indeed. Oh, yes!

Well, Sammie and Susie helped their mamma dip the eggs in the dye and stained them all sorts of pretty colors. Some were all one shade, and some were half one tint and half another, and then there were some all speckled with different colors, and these were very hard to make. Then, after they were all dry, Nurse Jane Fuzzy-Wuzzy, with her sharp teeth, just like chisels that a carpenter uses, drew pretty designs on the eggs; pictures of trees and birds and mountains and flowers and fairy castles and lakes and hills, and all sorts of things. Oh, they were the prettiest Easter eggs you ever saw!

"Here is the last egg," said Sammie. "May I dip this one in, mamma?"

"Yes," answered Mrs. Littletail, but she never would have let Sammie do it if she had known what was going to happen.

"I'll make this egg a skilligimink color," said Sammie, and he stood over the pot. Then, what do you think occurred? Why, Sammie leaned too far over and he fell right into that pot of skilligimink color; he and the egg together. And oh, dear me! what a time there was.

Sammie splashed around and splattered the skilligimink color all over the kitchen, and when his mamma and Susie fished him out of the pot he was dyed the most beautiful sky-blue-pink you ever saw! Oh, but he was a sight! The skilligimink color made him look like a piece of the rainbow.

"Oh, Sammie!" cried Susie, "how funny you look!"

And Sammie grunted:

"Huh! I guess it's nothing to laugh at!"

So they dried him with a towel, but the color didn't come off for ever so long, honest it didn't. But they had a lovely lot of Easter eggs, anyhow, so Sammie didn't mind much. Now, how about Hot Cross Buns next? Oh, of course, I mean a story about them.

Well you shall have it if the alarm clock will stop ringing its bell and making the back steps run to the front door.

STORY XXIII

SUSIE LITTLETAIL'S HOT CROSS BUNS

LET'S see where did we leave off last?

Oh, I remember now, it was about how Sammie fell down and hurt his nose, wasn't it? Oh, no, it wasn't either. It was about how he was colored sky-blue-pink; to be sure. Well, now I'm going to tell you about Hot Cross Buns, how Susie Littletail made some very especially fine ones, and what happened to them. But the last part is a secret, so I wish you wouldn't tell any one.

Susie was out skipping her grapevine rope, and thinking what a nice day it was, when her mamma called to her:

"Susie, don't you want to help Nurse Jane Fuzzy-Wuzzy make some Hot Cross Buns?"

"Of course," the little rabbit girl said, and, being a very kind little creature, she added: "Can Sammie help me, mamma?"

"Oh, I don't want to," said Sammie, who was playing marbles with Bully, the frog. They were using old hickory nuts and acorns for their marble shooters and agates in the ring. "I'm going to be a soldier or run an airplane or automobile when I grow up, so I don't want to learn to cook," said Sammie.

"Humph! I guess soldiers and automobile men and pilots are glad enough to eat when some one else cooks for them," said Nurse Jane Fuzzy-Wuzzy. "Anyhow, I can't have you mussing around my kitchen, Sammie, so Susie is the only one who can help me make Hot Cross Buns."

"Ask her if we can have the batter dishes and the one she mixes the chocolate frosting in, to clean out," prosed Bully, in a whisper, and when Sammie asked this of the nurse, who was also a cook, she said:

"Oh, I suppose so. But don't come around bothering while Susie and I are busy. I'll set the dishes out for you."

Then Sammie and Bully felt very good, for it's lots of fun to clean out the cake dishes when any one is baking, especially when Hot Cross Buns are being made. So the little boy rabbit and the little frog, who was such a good jumper, played marbles under the trees in the big woods.

Then Susie and Nurse Jane Fuzzy-Wuzzy went to work in the kitchen. First they took some flour, milk, eggs, sugar and whatever else goes into Hot Cross Buns, and mixed them all up in a big dish.

"Oh, my! How good that smells!" exclaimed Susie. "Won't Sammie and Bully be glad to get that?"

"Yes," said the nurse-cook. "But now we must make the frosting to go on top, and I think I'll mix in it some of the maple sugar that Uncle Wiggily made.

"Oh, fine!" exclaimed Susie, and she clapped her two front paws together, she was so glad.

So she and Nurse Jane Fuzzy-Wuzzy made a nice dish of maple-sugar frosting to go on top of the buns when they were baked.

"Now," said the cook, after a little while, "we must get the pans ready to bake the buns in. And, as we haven't much room in the kitchen, we will just set the dish of dough and the frosting out on the window sill, where they won't be in our way. As soon as we have the tins greased we will make the buns and put them right in the oven to bake."

So the nice, sweet, good-smelling and good-tasting batter and the dish of maple-sugar frosting were set outside on the window sill. Oh, how nice they smelled. It's a good thing that sly old fox wasn't around, I tell you!

Well, after a while, Sammie and Bully got

tired of playing marbles, and they walked around to the back of the underground house. And what do you think? Bully saw those dishes that had been set out on the window sill! Yes indeed, he saw them! Oh, he had sharp eyes, let me tell you!

"Look here!" Bully cried to Sammie. "They've put the stuff out for us. Oh, what a lot of it! Nice, sweet batter, and nice maple-sugar frosting. How kind they are."

"Do you s'pose all this is for us?" asked Sammie, who, whenever he cleaned out the baking dishes, had never seen so much as that in them.

"Of course it is," answered Bully. "Miss Fuzzy-Wuzzy said she'd put it out for us, and here it is out. Of course, it must be for us."

Well, Sammie thought so, too, after that, and then the little boy rabbit and Bully the frog sat down, with those two dishes, that had stuff in to make Hot Cross Buns, and they began to eat it all up. And after a while, when the batter was nearly all gone, who should come limping along but Uncle Wiggily Longears.

"Well, well," he said, just like that. "What have we here?"

Then Sammie told him how the good stuff had been left out by Nurse Jane Fuzzy-Wuzzy.

"My goodness me!" exclaimed the old rabbit, leaning on his cornstalk crutch, "how very odd."

"Would you like some?" asked Bully, the frog, very, very politely.

"Indeed I would," answered Uncle Wiggily Longears.

So they gave him some, and it tasted just as good as when he was a little boy rabbit.

But just as the last of the sweet batter and the maple-sugar frosting was eaten up, what should happen but that Jane Fuzzy-Wuzzy went to the window to take it in to bake, and of course it was gone.

Well, you should have seen how surprised she was. She was going to scold Sammie and Bully, only they said it was all a mistake. So they didn't get punished, and very luckily there was enough more stuff in the burrow pantry to make more Hot Cross Buns. So Jane Fuzzy-Wuzzy and Susie mixed up some, and these were soon baking in the oven. And, oh, how good they smelled, and they tasted as good as they smelled, each one with a maple-sugar cross on it. Now, next, if you would like me to, I'll tell you about hiding the Easter eggs.

But it will be jolly if you can stop the rubber ball pretending it is a fire engine and squirting water on the gold fish.

STORY XXIV

WHAT a lot of Easter eggs there were! I'm sure if you tried to count all that Sammie and Susie Littletail, and Papa and Mamma Littletail, to say nothing of Uncle Wiggily Longears and Nurse Jane Fuzzy-Wuzzy had colored, ready for Easter, you never could do it, never, never, never!

Of course, Uncle Wiggily couldn't get so very many of the eggs ready for the animal children, because, you know, he has rheumatism. But Sammie and Susie were so quick, and Nurse Jane Fuzzy-Wuzzy hurried so, that long before Easter Sunday morning, or Easter Monday morning, whenever children hunt for eggs, they were all ready to be found.

You see, the rabbits have also to hide all the Easter eggs that you children hunt for. Of course, I don't mean those eggs in the store windows; the pretty ones, made of candy, and with little windows that you look through to see beautiful scenes. Oh, no, not those, but the ones you

117

find at home. Those in the windows are put there by different kinds of rabbits.

Well, all the Easter eggs were ready, and Sammie and Susie, their papa and mamma, Uncle Wiggily Longears and Nurse Jane Fuzzy-Wuzzy, set out to hide them. There were many colors. I think I have told you about them, but I'll just mention a few again. There were red eggs, blue eggs, green eggs; pink, Alice-blue, Johnnie-red, Froggie-green, strawberry color, and then that new shade, skilligimink, which is very fine indeed, and which turned Sammie sky-blue-pink.

So the rabbits started off with their baskets of colored eggs on their paws.

"Now, be careful, Sammie," called his mamma. "Don't fall down and break any of those eggs."

"No, mamma," answered Sammie, who was still a little bit colored sky-blue-pink, for it hadn't all worn off yet. "I'll be very careful."

"So will I, mamma," called Susie.

So they walked on through the woods to visit Newark and East Orange and all the places around where children want Easter eggs. Of course, if you had gone out in the woods on top of Orange Mountain you could not have seen those rabbits, because they were invisible. That is, you couldn't see them, because Mrs. Cluck-Cluck, the hen lady, had given them all cloaks spun out of cobwebs, just like the Emperor of China once had, and this made it so no one could see them. For it would never do, you know, to have the rabbits spied upon when they are hiding the Easter eggs. It wouldn't be fair, any more than it would be right to peek when you're "it" in playing hide-and-go-seek.

Well, pretty soon, after a while, as they all walked through the woods, Sammie kept going slower and slower and slower, because his basket was quite heavy, until he was a long way behind his papa, his mamma and Susie. But he didn't mind that, for he knew he had plenty of time, when all at once who should come running out of the bushes but a great big dog. At first Sammie was frightened, but then when he looked again he knew the dog was not a rabbit-dog. No, what is worse, he was an egg-dog.

Now an egg-dog is a dog that eats eggs, and they are one of the very worst dogs there are. So the dog saw Sammie and knew what the little rabbit boy had in his basket. But the dog asked Sammie, making believe he didn't know:

"What have you in that basket, my fine little chap?" You see, the dog called Sammie "little chap" so as to pretend he was a friendly egg-dog.

"There are Easter eggs in the basket," said Sammie politely.

"And what, pray tell me, are Easter eggs, if I may be so bold as to ask?" inquired the dog, licking his teeth with his long red tongue, and blinking his eyes, as if he didn't care.

"Easter eggs," replied Sammie, "are eggs for children for Easter, and they are very prettily colored."

"Oh, ho!" exclaimed the dog, just like that, and he sniffed the air. "Please excuse me. But would you kindly be so good as to let me see those eggs? I never saw any colored ones."

"Well," answered Sammie, "I am in a hurry, but you may have one peep."

So he opened the top of the basket and there, surely enough, were the eggs, the green, the blue, the pink, the Johnnie red and the skilligimink colored ones and all.

"Oh, how lovely!" cried the bad egg-dog, sniffing the air again. "May I have one?"

"No," said Sammie, very decidedly, "these are for the little children."

Then that dog got angry. Oh, you should have seen how angry he got. No, on second thought I am glad you did not see how unpleasant he was, for it might spoil your Easter. Anyhow, he was dreadfully angry, dreadfully! He showed his teeth, and he made his hair stand up straight, and he growled:

"Give me all those eggs, or I'll take them right away from you! I am an egg-dog, and I must have eggs. Give them to me, I say!"

Well, poor Sammie was very much frightened! He trembled so that the eggs rattled together and very nearly were broken. Then he started to run away, but the bad dog ran after him, and what do you think? Just as the horrid creature was about to take those lovely Easter eggs out of the basket and eat them up, who should come flying through the woods but Mrs. Cluck-Cluck, the lady hen! She dashed at that dog, with her beak and her feathers sticking out, and made him run off. Then how glad Sammie was! He hurried and caught up to his papa and mamma, and soon all the Easter eggs were hidden for children to find on Easter morning.

Oh, what fun Sammie and Susie had running back through the woods after the eggs were all put in the secret places! Susie found a turnip in a field, and Sammie found a carrot, and they ate them as they hopped along.

Uncle Wiggily walked quite slowly, for his rheumatism was bothering him, and when those rabbits got home to the burrow, what do you think they found? Why, there were invitations for them all to come to a party that was going to be given by Lulu and Alice Wibblewobble. Alice and Lulu were little duck girls, and they lived with their papa and mamma, Mr. and Mrs. Wibblewobble, in a pen, not far from the rabbit burrow. They had a brother named Jimmie, but it wasn't his birthday, for he was a day older than his sisters, who were twins. That is, their birthdays came at the same time.

"May we go to the party, mamma?" asked Susie.

"Of course," answered Mamma Littletail, and they all went, even Nurse Jane Fuzzy-Wuzzy. They had a fine time, which I will tell you about later. But now I just want to mention one thing that occurred.

Just as the party was over, and every one was coming home, Uncle Wiggily, for a time, couldn't find his crutch, which Nurse Jane Fuzzy-Wuzzy had gnawed out of a cornstalk for him. Finally he found it behind the door. Then he, and Sammie and Susie, and Mr. and Mrs. Littletail started for the burrow.

Suddenly, all at once, when they were in the front yard of the Wibblewobble home, a silver trumpet sounded in the woods: "Ta-ra-ta-ra-ta-

ra!" just like that. Up came riding a little boy,
all in silver and gold, on a white horse. He
wanted to know if he was too late for the party,
the little boy did, and when Uncle Wiggily said
yes, the little boy was much disappointed.

Then Uncle Wiggily asked him who he was,
and the little boy said:

"I am the fairy prince! I used to be a mud
turtle, and live in the pond where Lulu and Alice
and Jimmie Wibblewobble swim. But I got tired
of being a mud turtle, though I *was* a fairy prince,
so I changed myself into a little boy."

But, do you know, Uncle Wiggily didn't believe him, and, what's more, the jolly old rabbit
gentleman said so. Oh, yes, indeed he did! Then
what did that little boy-fairy-prince do, but up
and say:

"Well, you soon will believe me, Uncle Wiggily. You come back to the woods a little later,
and something wonderful will happen. I'll make
you believe in fairies; that's what I will, for you
will see a red fairy very shortly."

But still Uncle Wiggily didn't believe, and he
went home, twinkling his pink nose and twiddling
his long ears at the same time.

But you just wait, for if I should happen to
find a penny rolling up hill, I will tell you, next,
about Uncle Wiggily and the red fairy.

Of course if you don't believe in fairies please
don't read the next story.   But if Peter Pan and
Tinker Bell believed in fairies, why can't you?
Anyhow why is it that rain drops are always wet?
Answer that if you please.

STORY XXV

UNCLE WIGGILY AND THE RED FAIRY

WELL, I didn't find that penny rolling up hill, after all, but never mind, I'll tell you a story just the same. Let's see, we left off about Uncle Wiggily Longears, the old gentleman rabbit, and what was going to happen to him when he should meet the red fairy, didn't we?

Uncle Wiggily walked along very slowly, going home from the party Lulu and Alice Wibble-wobble had given. Sammie Littletail saw how slowly his uncle walked, and asked:

"What is the matter, Uncle Wiggily? Does your rheumatism hurt you very much?"

"No, it isn't that," replied the old gentleman rabbit, "though it does pain me some. I was just wondering about that red fairy."

"Oh, do you really suppose one will appear, as the fairy prince said?" asked Susie, making her nose twinkle like two stars and a comet on a frosty night.

"No," spoke Uncle Wiggily very decidedly,

125

"I don't really believe one will.   Still, there may.
You never can tell in this world what is going to
happen."   And I think Uncle Wiggily was right
about that, don't you?

"Oh!" cried Susie, "I wish I could come with
you, Uncle Wiggily.   I never saw a real fairy
in all my life.   Couldn't I come with you?" and
the little rabbit girl went close to her uncle, and
took hold of his crutch, gnawed by the muskrat,
Nurse Jane Fuzzy-Wuzzy, out of a cornstalk.

"Yes, I suppose you could," answered Susie's
uncle, who was very kind to her.

"Oh, no!" exclaimed Sammie.   "It might spoil
the magic spell, if more than one went, Uncle
Wiggily.   Maybe the fairy would not like it.
You had better go alone."

"All right," answered the old gentleman rabbit,
"anything to please you.   I'll go alone."

Well, when the rabbit family got back to their
burrow, after the party, they could talk of nothing else but what was going to happen when
Uncle Wiggily should meet the red fairy.   Sammie and Susie didn't want to go to bed, they were
so excited, but their mamma sent them up with
Nurse Jane Fuzzy-Wuzzy.

Now listen very carefully, for the fairy will
soon appear, and you know what happens then.
Oh, yes, indeed, something wonderful.

Well, when it came time, Uncle Wiggily started off alone to the woods to meet the red fairy. He walked on, and on, and on, and he had to go pretty slowly, because his rheumatism was hurting him again.

And suddenly, when he was right under a big oak tree, what should he hear but a silver trumpet blowing "Ta-ra-ta-ra-ta-ra!" Just like that, honest. Then he stood still, and a sort of shivery feeling came over him, and he looked up and he looked down and he looked to one side and then to the other. And then he wiggled his ears, and he twinkled his pink nose as fast as fast could be. Then he heard some one call:

"Uncle Wiggily Longears!"

"Yes, I'm here!" he answered.

"And I am the red fairy!" cried the voice again, and when the old gentleman rabbit looked up in the tree, what do you suppose he saw?

There, perched on a limb, was a beautiful little lady, all dressed in red, with a red cloak on, and a red hat on, and the hat had a red feather in it; in fact, the little lady was as red as Red Riding Hood ever thought of being.

"Do you believe in fairies, Uncle Wiggily?" she asked.

"No," replied the old rabbit, "I can't say that I do."

"Well," went on the little creature, "you soon will. Watch me carefully."

And with that, what did she do but float down from that tall tree, just as one of those red balloons you buy at the circus floats along. Yes, sir, she floated right down to where Uncle Wiggily stood. Then she waved her magic wand in the air three times, and said this word: "Higgildy-piggilyhobbledehoi!" It's a very hard word for you to say, I know, but easy for a fairy. Well, she said that word, and then, all at once, what should happen but that a golden ball appeared, floating in the air.

"Catch the golden ball!" cried the red fairy.

"I can't!" answered the old rabbit. "I haven't played ball in years, and years, and years."

"Well," went on the fairy, with a laugh, "no matter. It will come to you." And you may not believe me, but that golden ball floated right down into Uncle Wiggily's paws. He had to drop his crutch to catch the golden ball.

"Now," said the red lady, "do you want to see me do something magical to prove that I am wonderful, and a real fairy?"

"Yes," answered Uncle Wiggily, "certainly. Go ahead. I dare you!"

"Well, what shall I do? Name something wonderful," said the red lady.

"If you could cure my rheumatism it would be wonderful," answered Uncle Wiggily. "It hurts me something fierce, now."

"Ha! That is not wonderful at all," spoke the red fairy. "That is altogether too easy. But I will do it all the same. Watch me carefully."

Then, as true as I'm telling you, that golden ball began to dance up and down, and sideways, and around and around. Uncle Wiggily began leaping here, and there, and everywhere, until he could hardly see the ball. And the silver trumpet blew: "Ta-ra-ta-ra-ta-ra!" just like that, and all of a sudden, Uncle Wiggily felt himself being lifted up, and whirled around, and then came a clap of thunder, and then all was still and quiet, and a little bird began to sing. Then the fairy's voice asked:

"Well, Uncle Wiggily, how is your rheumatism now?"

"Why!" exclaimed the old rabbit in great surprise, "it is all gone. It certainly is. I never would have believed it."

And, honestly, his pain was all gone, and he didn't need his crutch for a long time after that.

Then Uncle Wiggily believed that the red lady was a fairy, and he hurried home to tell Sammie and Susie, while the little red lady and the golden ball flew back into the tree.

"Oh!" cried Susie, when she heard the story, "I wish I could see a fairy!"

And she did! The very next day. And, if nothing happens, the story after this one will be about Susie Littletail and the blue fairy.

But not if the roller skate takes one of the auto's wheels to play jacks with and forgets to bring it back.

STORY XXVI

SUSIE AND THE BLUE FAIRY

THEY were talking about Uncle Wiggily's visit to the red fairy, in the rabbits' burrow the next day, when Susie remarked:

"Well, if I saw a fairy, I think I'd ask for something more magical than just having my rheumatism cured."

"No you wouldn't," said her uncle, as he nibbled a bit of chocolate-covered carrot that Nurse Jane Fuzzy-Wuzzy had made. "You think you would, but you wouldn't. In the first place, you never had rheumatism, or you'd be glad to get the first fairy you saw to cure it. And in the second place, when you see a fairy it makes you feel so funny you don't know what you are saying. But I am certainly glad I met that one. I never felt better in all my life than I do since my rheumatism is cured. I believe I'll dance a jig."

"Oh, no, don't," begged Mamma Littletail.

"Yes, I shall too," spoke Uncle Wiggily. "Begging your pardon, of course, Alvinah."

You see, Mamma Littletail's first name was Alvinah. So Uncle Wiggily danced a jig, and did it fairly well, considering everything.

That afternoon Susie Littletail went for a walk in the woods. She was all alone, for Sammie had gone over to play with Bully, the frog, and Billie and Johnnie Bushytail, his squirrel chums. Susie walked along, and she was rather hoping she might meet the fairy prince, who was changed from a mud turtle into a nice boy, and who wanted to come to Lulu and Alice Wibblewobble's party. But Susie didn't meet him, and, when it began to get dark, she started for home.

"Oh!" Susie exclaimed aloud, as she came to a little spot where the grass grew nice and green, and where the trees were all set in a circle, just as if they were playing, Ring Around the Rosey, Sweet Tobacco Posey.

"Oh, dear, I wish I would meet with a fairy, as Uncle Wiggily did! But I don't s'pose I ever will. I never have any good luck! Only last week I lost my ring with the blue stone in it."

And just then—oh, in fact, right after Susie finished speaking, what should she hear but a voice singing. Yes, a voice singing; a sweet, silvery voice, and this is what it sang. Of course, I can't sing this in a sweet, silvery voice, but I'll do the best I can. Now this is the song:

"If any one is seeking
   A fairy for to see,
If they will kindly glance up
   Into this chestnut tree
They'll see what they are seeking,
   I'm truly telling you,
For I'm a little fairy
   All dressed in baby-blue."

Then, you may believe me or not, Susie looked up into the tree, and there, in a hole where an Owl once lived, was a really and truly-ruly fairy. Honest!

Susie knew at once it was a fairy that she saw because the little creature was colored baby blue—you know, the shade they put on babies—and she had gauzy wings, with stars on them, and carried a magic wand which also had a star on it.

Still, the little rabbit girl wanted to make sure, so she asked: "Are you a fairy?"

"I am," replied the little creature in blue. "Now I'll ask you a question. Can you kindly tell me how much two and two are?"

"Four," answered Susie.

"Is it really?"

"Of course. You ought to know that," spoke Susie proudly, for she was at the head of her arithmetic class.

"Ought I?" asked the fairy with a sigh. "Well, I suppose I ought, but I haven't been to school in ever so long—not since I was a wee bit of a child, and that's ever and ever so many years ago, when I was no bigger than that," and she pointed to something in the air.

"Bigger than what?" asked Susie, who didn't see anything.

"Than that speck of star dust," went on the blue fairy. "It's so small you can't see it. But no matter. Because you were so kind as to tell me how much two and two are, I will give you three wishes."

"Will you, really?" cried Susie in delight.

"Yes, three wishes, for I am a regular fairy, and that is the regular number of wishes you may have. Some fairies allow only two wishes, and some only one. But I always allow three. Go ahead now, and wish."

"Let me see," thought Susie, and her nose twinkled like three stars, she was so excited. "First I wish for a golden coach drawn by four big ducks."

"Oh!" cried the fairy, "I'm so sorry; for wishes like that, though they come true, never last. Still, you may have it," and she waved her magic wand, and the golden coach and four ducks appeared right there in the woods—honest! "Wish again,

my dear," went on the fairy, and this time Susie
was more careful.

"I wish for ten boxes of chocolate-covered carrots," she said, and once more the fairy said she
was sorry, for that wish wouldn't last. Still, it
came true, and down from the tree where the blue
fairy sat, came tumbling the ten boxes of chocolate-covered carrots, each one wrapped in lace
paper. Susie put them in the golden coach, and
was ready for her next wish. She thought a good
long while over this one. Then she said:

"I wish I could find my ring with the blue
stone!"

At that the fairy clapped her tiny hands. "That
is a fine wish!" she cried. "It will come true, and
stay true. But the other wishes—" and she shook
her head sorrowfully.

Then she waved her magic wand three times in
the air, and suddenly, in less than two jumps, the
ring with the blue stone, that Susie had lost, appeared right on the end of the wand. And it flew
off and landed right on Susie's paw. Oh, wasn't
she glad!

Then the fairy said:

"The ring will last, because that is blue, and I
am blue, too. Now, good bye, Susie."

With that she disappeared, changing into a
butterfly with golden wings.

Then Susie started to get in the golden coach and ride home, but, would you believe me, those ducks ran away, upsetting the coach and breaking it, and scattering the ten boxes of chocolate-covered carrots all over. Oh, how badly Susie felt!

But it was just what the fairy said would happen. The first two wishes didn't last. Anyhow, Susie had the ring, and she hurried home to tell her story.

Now, if the lawn mower doesn't cut all the hair off the dusting brush you shall hear next about Sammie and the green fairy.

STORY XXVII

SAMMIE AND THE GREEN FAIRY

WHEN Susie told her brother Sammie about what happened to her in the woods, when she saw the blue fairy, the little rabbit boy remarked:

"Aw, I guess you fell asleep and dreamed that, Susie," for that's the way with brothers sometimes. I once had a brother, and he—but there, I'll tell you about him some other time.

"No," answered Susie, "I didn't dream it. Why, here's my ring to prove it," and she held out the ring with the blue stone in it.

"I guess you found that in the woods, where you lost it," went on Sammie. "I don't believe in fairies at all."

"But didn't one cure Uncle Wiggily's rheumatism?"

"Aw, well, I guess his rheumatism would have gotten better anyhow."

"It wouldn't, so there!" exclaimed Susie. "I just hope you see a fairy some day, and I hope they don't treat you as kind as the one treated me, even if the ducks did run away from me and disappear."

Of course Susie didn't really want anything bad to happen to her brother. But you just wait and see what did happen. Oh, it was something, very, very strange, yes, indeed, and I'm not fooling a bit; no, indeed. I wouldn't make it out anything different than what it really was, not for a penny and a half.

Well, it happened about a week later. Sammie was coming home from a ball game, which he had played with Johnnie and Billie Bushytail (of whom I shall tell you later), and some others of his chums, and he was in a deep, dark part of the wood, when, suddenly, he heard a crashing in the bushes.

"Pooh!" exclaimed Sammie. "I s'pose that's one of the fairies. I'm not going to notice her," and with that he tossed his baseball up in the air, careless like, to show that he didn't mind. But he was a bit nervous, all the same, and his hand slipped and his best ball went right down in a deep, dark, muddy puddle of water. Then Sammie felt pretty sad, I tell you, and he was going to get a stick to fish the ball out, when he heard the crashing in the bushes again, and what should appear—no, not a fairy, but a bad, ugly fox.

"Ah!" exclaimed the fox, looking at Sammie,

and smacking his lips, "I've been waiting for you
for some time."

"Yes?" asked the little boy rabbit.   "So what
do you want?"

Sammie tried to see a way to run past that fox,
only there wasn't any.

"Yes, really," went on the fox.   "Have you had
your supper?"

"No," replied Sammie, "I haven't."

"Neither have I," continued the fox, "but I'm
going to have it pretty soon; in fact, almost immediately," which you children know means right
away.   "I'm going to eat directly," went on that
bad fox, and he smacked his lips again and looked
at Sammie, as if he were going to eat him up, for
that's really what he meant when he said he was
going to have supper.

Oh, how frightened Sammie was.   He began
to tremble, and he wished he had started for home
earlier.   Then the fox crouched down and was
just going to jump on that little boy rabbit, when
something happened.

Right up from that puddle of water, where
Sammie had lost his ball, sprang a little man in
green.   He was green all over, like Bully, the
frog, but the funny part of it was that he wasn't
wet a bit, even though he came up out of the
water.

"Ha! What have we here?" he cried out, just like that.

"If—if you please, sir," began Sammie, "I——"

"It's my supper time!" cried the fox, interrupting, which was not very polite on his part. "It's my supper time, and I'm hungry."

"I don't see anything to eat," spoke the little green man. "Nothing at all," and he looked all around.

"If—if you please, kind sir," went on Sammie, "I think he intends to eat me."

"What! What!" cried the little green man. "The very idea! The very idonical idea! We'll see about that! Oh, my, yes, and a bushel of apple turnovers besides! Aha! Ahem!"

Then he looked most severely at that fox, most severely, I do assure you, and he asked: "Were you going to eat up my friend Sammie Littletail?"

"I was, but I didn't know he was a friend of yours," replied the fox, beginning to tremble. Oh, you could see right away that he was afraid of that little green man.

"Oh, you bad fox, you!" cried the little green man. "Oh, you bad fox! Just for that I'm going to turn you into a little country village! Presto, chango! Smacko, Mackeo! Bur-r-r-r!"

and he waved his hands at the fox, who immediately disappeared. And the fox was changed into a little country village, with a church, a school and thirty-one houses, and it's called Foxtown to this very day. I ought to know, for I used to live there.

"Well, Sammie?" asked the little green man, when the fox had vanished, "How do you feel now?"

"Much better, kind sir. Thank you. But who are you?"

"Me? Who am I? Why, don't you know?"

"No, indeed, unless you're some relation to Bully, the frog."

"Well, I am a sort of distant thirty-second cousin to him. I am the green fairy. And to prove it, look here, I will get your ball back for you," said the little man.

Then while Sammie looked on, his eyes getting bigger and bigger and his breath coming faster and faster, until it was like a locomotive or a choo-choo, whatever you call them, going up hill, that little green man waved his hands over that puddle of water, where Sammie's ball had fallen. And he spoke the magic word, which must never be spoken except on Friday nights, so if you read this on any night but Friday you must skip it, and wait. The word is (Tirratarratorratarratirratarratum), and I put it in brackets, so there would be no mistake.

Well, all of a sudden, after the magic word was spoken, Sammie's ball came bounding up out of that water, and it was as dry as a wringer, and it had on a nice, new, clean, white cover.

"There," said the little green man proudly, "I guess that's doing some tricks in the fairy line, isn't it?"

"It certainly is," agreed Sammie, "I can't thank you enough."

"Just believe in fairies after this," said the little green man, as he changed into a bumble bee and flew off.

Now, how would you like to hear about Susie and the fairy godmother next?

You shall if the cough drop doesn't catch cold so it can't go to the movies.

STORY XXVIII

SUSIE AND THE FAIRY GODMOTHER

YOU can just imagine how excited Susie and her mamma and papa and Nurse Jane Fuzzy-Wuzzy were when Sammie hopped home and told about the bad fox who had been changed into a country village. Uncle Wiggily Longears was surprised, too. He said:

"My, it does seem to me there are strange goings on in these woods. There never used to be any fairies here. I wonder where they come from?"

"Well, it's a good thing that fox has been changed into a village," spoke Papa Littletail. "If he hadn't been, I would have had him arrested for frightening you, Sammie. I know the Police Dog down at our corner, and I'm sure he would have arrested the fox for me. But it's all right now," and Sammie's papa sat back in his chair and read the paper, for he was tired that night from working in the turnip factory. You see, he had changed from the carrot factory, and had a job sorting turnips. And sometimes he would bring little sweet turnips home to the rabbit children.

One day Susie was hurrying back from the store with a loaf of bread, a yeast cake and three-and-a-half pounds of granulated sugar, and she was sort of wondering if she would meet the blue fairy again when, just as she got opposite a place where some goldenrod grew, she heard a voice saying:

"Oh, dear! Oh, dear me! I shall never be able to reach it! Never, never, never!"

Susie looked around, and saw a nice, little old lady, trying to break off a stem of goldenrod.

"Oh, dear me suz-dud!" cried the old lady again, and then Susie saw that she was very little indeed, hardly larger than a ten-cent plate of ice cream after it's all melted. Of course the old lady couldn't reach the goldenrod, she was so little.

"What is the matter?" asked Susie very politely. "Can I help you?"

"Thank you, my dear child," went on the little old lady. "If you would be so kind as to reach me down a stem of goldenrod, I would be very much obliged to you."

"What do you want with it?" asked Susie, wondering who the little old lady could possibly be.

"Why, I want it for a fairy wand," she answered. "I have lost mine."

"Are you a fairy, too?" asked the little rabbit girl, and she began to wonder what would happen next as she broke off a stem of goldenrod and gave it to the old lady.

"Indeed I am," was the answer. "I am a fairy godmother. I have charge of all the other fairies, the blue fairy and the red fairy and the green fairy, and all the other colors, including the fairy prince, who used to be a mud turtle."

"But, if you are a fairy," asked Susie, "why couldn't you make that goldenrod come down to you, when you weren't tall enough to reach up to it?"

"Hush!" exclaimed the fairy godmother, for she really was one, as you shall see. "Hush, my dear child! It's a great secret. Don't tell any one," and she put her right hand over her mouth and her left hand over one ear, and held the goldenrod under her arm. "You see, I lost my magic wand," she went on, "and I couldn't do any more magic until I got a new one. Now I am all right, and to reward you, you may come with me."

"But I have to get home with the bread and sugar and yeast cake," said Susie.

"No," spoke the fairy godmother, "you will not need to be in a hurry. Besides, what I will show

you will happen in an instant, and you will get
home in time after all.''

So she waved the goldenrod in the air, and once
more the silver trumpet sounded: "Ta-ra-ta-ra-
ta-ra!'' and, all of a sudden, Susie found herself
lifted up, and she and the fairy godmother were
sailing right through the air on a big burdock
leaf. At first Susie was afraid, but she soon got
over her fright and enjoyed the ride.

"Where are we going?'' she asked.

"We are going to where the fairies live,'' answered the little old woman, but she seemed larger
now, and the old dress she had worn had changed
into a cloak of gold and silver with diamonds and
rubies sprinkled on it all over, like frost in the
grass on a cold morning.

So pretty soon—oh, I guess in about as long as
it would take to eat a peanut, or, maybe, two,
Susie and the old lady reached fairyland. At
least that's what Susie thought it was, for there
were fairies all about. The red fairy was there,
and the green, and the blue fairies.

And the blue fairy asked: "Have you your
ring yet, Susie?'' Then Susie said she had, but
she didn't want to talk any more, for so many
wonderful things were going on.

The fairies were skipping about, leaping here

and there, some riding on the backs of birds and butterflies and bumblebees, and some running in and out of holes in the ground.

"What are they doing?" asked Susie, moving her long ears back and forth. She and the fairy godmother had alighted from the burdock leaf.

"They are doing kind things to the people of the earth," replied the fairy godmother, "and it keeps them busy, let me tell you."

Then Susie saw fairies doing all sorts of magical tricks, such as making lemonade out of lemons, and things like that.

Then, all at once, just when one little fairy was making a hat out of some straw, the godmother said: "It is time for us to go now," so the burdock leaf came sailing back through the air, and Susie got on. As they came near the woods where the goldenrod grew they saw a boy throwing a stone at a robin.

"Ah, I must stop that!" cried the fairy godmother, so she waved her new magic wand that Susie had helped her get, and that stone turned right around in the air, and instead of hitting the bird, it flew back and hit that boy on the end of his nose! Oh, how he cried, and, what is better, he never threw stones at birds again. I call that a pretty good trick, don't you?

Well, the burdock leaf fluttered to the ground, and Susie ran home, and she was just in time to help her mother bake the bread.

The next story is going to be about Uncle Wiggily and the fairy spectacles. That is, I think it is, but, if you like, you may turn the page to make sure. But you are only allowed just one peep, only one, mind you. Because if you peep twice the goldfish may turn into a canary bird and then what will happen?

STORY XXIX

UNCLE WIGGILY AND THE FAIRY SPECTACLES

SAMMIE and Susie Littletail were playing out in front of their burrow. Their mamma had a headache, and had gone to lie down in a dark room, and Nurse Jane Fuzzy-Wuzzy had put a mustard leaf on the back of Mamma Littletail's neck, for that is sometimes good for a headache.

"What shall we do?" asked Susie.

"Oh, I don't know," replied her brother. "S'pose we play stump tag?"

"All right; you're 'it,' Sammie," called Susie.

So Sammie began to hop after Susie. You see, when you play stump tag you have to keep on a stump if you don't want to be tagged. It's lots of fun. Try it some day, if you can find a place where there are plenty of stumps. Well, after playing this game for some time, the rabbit children grew tired. Then they played other games, and they were making quite a noise, when Uncle Wiggily Longears came out.

"You children will have to make less racket,"

he said, real cross like. "Your mamma has a headache."

Then Sammie and Susie were quieter for a time, but soon they were almost as noisy as before.

"Now you must run right away from here!" cried Uncle Wiggily, coming to the door of the underground house again, and he spoke still more crossly.

"What do you s'pose ails Uncle Wiggily?" asked Susie, as she and Sammie hopped away.

"I don't know," replied Sammie, "unless it's his rheumatism again."

"No, it can't be that. Don't you remember, the red fairy cured him?"

"Maybe it came back."

"Oh, no, fairies don't do things that way. I guess he must have indigestion. But I wish he wouldn't be so cross, especially when mamma has a headache and Nurse Jane Fuzzy-Wuzzy can't come out to play with us. Oh, dear! Isn't it too bad?"

"What's too bad?" asked a little voice, under a big clump of grass, and at that moment out came walking a little pink fairy. Oh, she was the dearest little thing you ever saw! I just wish I could take you to see her, but it's not allowed. Some day, perhaps—but there, I must get on with the

story.   Well, the little pink fairy stood out in the
sunlight, and she asked again: "What is the matter?"

"Oh," explained Susie, who, by this time, had
gotten used to fairies of all kinds, "mamma has a
headache, and Uncle Wiggily is cross."

"Headache, eh?   Uncle Wiggily cross?   Perhaps his glasses do not fit him," suggested the
fairy.

"Oh, I guess there's nothing the matter with
his spectacles," answered Sammie.   "I saw him
reading a book with them."

"You never can tell," declared the pink fairy.
"Suppose you call him out here, and we'll take a
look at his glasses.   Maybe he has the wrong
kind."

"What about mamma's headache?" asked Susie.

"Oh!   I'll stop that in a minute," replied the
fairy kindly, so she waved her magic wand in the
air three times.   "Now your mamma's head is all
better," she added.

And, surely enough, when Susie ran in the burrow to ask Uncle Wiggily to come out, Mamma
Littletail's head was all well.   Wasn't that just
fine?

Well, at first Uncle Wiggily didn't want to
come out.   He was still cross, but finally Susie

begged him so hard that he did. He saw the little pink fairy, and he asked, real cross like: "Well, what do you want of me?"

"Aha!" exclaimed the pink fairy. "I see what the trouble is. It's your spectacles."

"They're all right," growled Uncle Wiggily.

"They are not," declared the fairy very decidedly. "Let me look at them," and before you could say "Pussy-cat Mole jumped over a coal," she frisked those glasses off Uncle Wiggily's nose. "Oh!" she cried, "look here, Sammie and Susie! What terribly gloomy spectacles!"

Then she held them up, first in front of Sammie, and then in front of Susie. And when they looked through the glasses the little rabbit children saw that everything was dark, and gloomy, and dreary, and even the sun seemed to be behind a cloud. Oh, it was as cold and unpleasant as it is just before a snowstorm.

"No wonder you were cross!" said the fairy. "But I will soon fix that! Presto-chango! Ring around the rosey, sweet tobacco posey!" she cried, and then she rubbed first one pink finger on one glass, and then another pink finger on the other glass of the spectacles.

And a most wonderful thing happened. The fairy smiled as she held the glasses up in front of Sammie and Susie, and as true as I'm telling you, everything was as bright and shining as a new tin dishpan. Oh, everything looked lovely! The flowers were gay, and the sun shone, and even the green grass was sort of pink, while the sky was rose-colored.

"There," said the fairy to Uncle Wiggily. "Try your glasses now, please."

So Uncle Wiggily Longears put on his glasses again, and he cried out:

"Why, goodness me! Oh, my suz-dud! Oh, turnips and carrots and a chocolate cake! Oh, my goodness me!"

"What's the matter?" asked Susie.

"Why, everything looks different," answered her uncle. "Oh, how much better I feel! Whoop-de-doodle-do!" and he began to dance a jiggity-jig. "Who would have thought my glasses were so dark and gloomy?" he went on. "I feel ever so much better, now. Come on, Sammie and Susie, and I'll buy you some cabbage ice cream. And you too, little pink fairy."

You see, he had been looking through gloomy glasses all that while, and that was what made him cross.

"Oh, thank you, I only eat rose-leaf ice cream," the fairy said. "But I'm not hungry now. Good-luck to all of you, and may you be always happy!" Then she turned into a little bird and

flew away singing, while Uncle Wiggily and the
rabbit children hopped to the ice cream store.
Now, unless I'm much mistaken, the next story
will be about Sammie and how he saved Billie
Bushytail.   But of course you never can tell
what will happen; especially if the coffee pot goes
to a party and doesn't come home in time for
breakfast.

STORY XXX

SAMMIE SAVES BILLIE BUSHYTAIL

SAMMIE LITTLETAIL was out in a green field digging a burrow, or underground house. He didn't really need another house, for the one he, and his papa, and mamma, and sister, lived in was very nice, but, as he had nothing else to do, he thought he would dig a big hole, and, maybe, go all the way through to China. Sammie thought he would like to see how China looked, and he thought he might make the acquaintance of some Chinese rabbits.

Well, he hadn't gotten down very far, and he was still a good many miles from China, when he heard some one singing a song in a very loud voice. Now I don't advise you to sing it quite so loudly, for you might awaken the baby, if you have one in your house. Anyway, it does just as well to sing it softly. This is the song Sammie heard:

> "I want to be a sailor
> And sail the ocean blue.

I'd journey to a distant land
  And then come back to you.
I'd bring you lots of happiness,
  A big trunk filled with joy;
A barrel full of lollypops
  For every girl or boy."

Well, when Sammie heard that he cried out:
"Is that a fairy?"

"No," was the answer.

"Oh, then you must be Billie or Johnnie Bushytail," went on Sammie, for he remembered that
once the little boy squirrels went sailing and were
shipwrecked.

"Yes, I'm Billie," said the voice, and then up
popped the little squirrel. "But what did you say
about a fairy?" he asked.

"I thought at first you were a fairy," continued
Sammie, and then he stopped digging the hole in
the ground. "There have been such a lot of
fairies around here lately," Sammie added. "Red
ones, and green ones, and blue ones, and——"

"Are you talking about Easter eggs or something else?" inquired Billie Bushytail.

"Fairies, of course."

"Oh, get out! Oh, ho! Don't tell me that!
Why, how superfluous!" cried Billie, for that last
was a new word he had just learned. "Don't
mention fairies to me!" he continued.

"Why not?" Sammie wanted to know.

"Because I don't believe there are such things!" cried Billie, frisking his big tail until it looked like a dusting brush they use after sweeping to knock the dust from the furniture onto the floor again. "Don't talk to me like that, Sammie," said Billie.

"Well," remarked the little boy rabbit, "all I've got to say is there *are* fairies! But where's Johnnie? Maybe he believes in 'em."

"No, he doesn't. Besides he's gone out walking with Sister Sallie. Come on, let's have a catch. Where's your ball?"

"I didn't bring it," replied Sammie. "But we can have some fun playing in this hole I've dug."

So Sammie and Billie played for some time, and pretty soon, oh, in about two and a half frisks of Billie's tail, what should happen, but that, all of a sudden, a great big hawk swooped down from the sky and grabbed that little boy squirrel up in its claws, and flew off with him. Well, you can just imagine how scared Sammie was. His nose twinkled so fast he sneezed three times. Then he looked up, and there was the hawk, flying away, and away, and away with poor Billie. Oh, wasn't it dreadful!

"Save me! Save me!" Billie cried from up there among the clouds.

"I will! I will!" shouted Sammie, and then he got so excited that he ran around in a circle, and tried to catch his tail, but it was so short that he couldn't even see it, no matter how fast he went around. Then he grabbed up a stone, and he threw it at that hawk, but of course he couldn't hit him, for the big, bad bird was too far away.

"Oh, whatever shall I do?" exclaimed Sammie. "If I could only fly, I'd go up after that hawk. Oh, why didn't Susie wish for wings for me and her instead of for a golden chariot and ten boxes of chocolate-covered carrots the time she saw the blue fairy? Oh, why didn't she? Wings would have been of some use!"

Then Sammie ran around after his tail some more, but he couldn't get it, and the hawk kept taking Billie farther and farther away, and then Sammie cried out: "Oh, dear! Oh, dear! Oh, dear!" three times, just like that. Then, all at once, the little green man suddenly appeared. He always appears when any one says "Oh, dear!" three times in exactly the right way, but it's hard to know just what is the right way.

"Well," said the little green man, "you seem to be in trouble."

"I am," cried Sammie. "A hawk has caught Billie Bushytail, and I want to save him."

"Very well," said the little green man, "since you are so kind, you shall save him. Shut your eyes, cross your front paws, and wrinkle your

nose three times and a half." So Sammie did
this, and in another instant, the little green man
changed into a big, kind, good-natured eagle.
"Get up on my back," the eagle said to Sammie,
"and we will save Billie."

So Sammie got on the eagle's back, and the
big bird flew after that hawk, and, pretty soon, it
caught up to him.

"Here, you let Billie Bushytail go!" cried Sammie, and then he took a long stick he had grabbed
up, and he hit that hawk. At first the hawk
wasn't going to let go of the little squirrel, but
when the eagle bit him three times on each leg,
then that bad hawk bird was glad enough to drop
Billie and fly off. Oh, my, no, he didn't drop
Billie to the ground; that would have been too
bad. He only dropped him on the eagle's back,
where Sammie was, and pretty soon the two little
animal boys were safe on the ground once more,
and the eagle had turned into a little green man
again.

"I'm ever so much obliged to you for saving
me, Sammie," spoke Billie.

"Oh, I couldn't have done it if it hadn't been for
the green fairy," replied Sammie, and of course
he couldn't.

Then Billie thanked the little man very kindly,
and he felt sorry for not believing in fairies, and

he said he would try to, after that.   So the boy
squirrel and the boy rabbit played together some
more, until it was time to go home.

Next I'll tell you about Susie and the fairy
carrot, that is if the ham sandwich doesn't run
away from the mustard at the dill pickle's party.

STORY XXXI

SUSIE AND THE FAIRY CARROT

SUSIE and Sammie Littletail had gone to the woods for a walk, and to gather some flowers, for they expected company at the underground house, and they wanted it to look pretty. Mr. and Mrs. Bushytail and Billie and Johnnie and Sister Sallie were coming, and Susie and her brother hoped to have a very nice time.

Well, they wandered on, and on, and on, and had gathered quite a number of flowers, when Sammie said:

"Come on, we've got enough; let's go home."

"No," answered Susie, "I want to get some sky-blue-pink flowers. I think they are so pretty."

"I don't," answered her brother, for that color always reminded him of the time he fell in the dye pot, when they were coloring Easter eggs. "I'm going home. Yellow, and red, and blue, and white flowers are good enough. I don't want any fancy colors."

161

"Well, you go home and I'll come pretty soon,"
said his sister. So while Sammie turned back, the
little rabbit girl kept on. Oh, I don't know how
far she went, but it was a good distance, I'm sure,
but still she couldn't seem to find that sky-blue-
pink flower. She looked everywhere for it, high
and low, and even sideways, which is a very good
place; but she couldn't find it. And she kept on
going, hoping every minute the flower would happen to be behind a stump or under a bush. But
no, it wasn't.

And then, all of a sudden, about as quick as
you can shut your eyes and open them again, Susie was lost! Yes, lost in those woods all alone.
She looked all around, and she didn't know where
she was. She'd never been so far away from home
before, and, oh, how frightened she was!

But she was a brave little rabbit girl, and she
didn't cry, that is, at first. She started to try to
find her way back, but the more she tried the more
lost she became, until she was all turned around,
you know, like when they blindfold you and turn
you around three times before they let you try to
pin the tail on the cloth donkey at a party. Yes,
that's how it was.

Well, then Susie began to cry, and I don't
blame her a bit. I think I would do the same
myself. Susie sat down and cried. Then she felt

hungry and she looked around for something to eat, and what should she see, right there in the woods, but a carrot.

"Oh!" she cried, "how lucky! Now I shan't be hungry, anyhow." So she picked up the carrot and started to eat it, when all at once that carrot spoke to her. What's that? You don't see how a carrot could speak? Well, it did all the same. You just listen, please, and maybe you'll see how it happened.

"Please don't eat me," the carrot said, in a squeaky voice.

"Why not?" asked Susie, who was very much surprised.

"Because I am a fairy carrot," it went on. Now do you see how it could speak? Well, I guess! "Yes, I am a fairy carrot, Susie, and I can help you. What do you want most?" the fairy carrot asked.

"I want to find my way home," said the little rabbit girl.

"Very well, my dear," went on the vegetable. "Place me on the ground in front of you, stand on your hind legs, wiggle your left ear, and see what happens."

So Susie did this, and would you believe me, for I'm not exaggerating the least bit, that fairy carrot rolled along on the ground in front of Susie.

"Follow, follow, follow me,
  And you soon at home will be,"

the carrot said, in a sing-song voice, and it rolled
on, still more, and Susie followed.

First the carrot went through a deep, dark
part of the woods, but Susie wasn't at all afraid,
for she believed in fairies. Then, pretty soon, the
carrot came to a great big hole. It was too big to
jump over, and too deep to crawl down into, and
too wide to run around.

"Oh, dear!" cried Susie, "I don't see how I'm
going to get over this." But do you s'pose that
carrot was bothered? No, sir; not the least bit.
It stretched out, like a piece of rubber, and thrust
itself across that hole until it was a regular little
bridge, and Susie could walk safely over. Then
it became an ordinary fairy carrot again, and
rolled on in front of the little rabbit girl showing
her just which way to go.

After a while Susie came to a great big lake,
one she had never seen before.

"Oh, how shall we get over this?" cried Susie.

"Don't worry," spoke the carrot. Then it
turned into a little boat, and Susie got into it, and
sailed over that lake as nicely as you please.
Then the carrot turned into an ordinary, garden,
fairy carrot again, and rolled on, Susie following.

Pretty soon they came to a place where the woods and brush were all on fire.

"Oh, I know we shall never get over that place!" exclaimed Susie, for she was very much afraid of fire, because she had once burned a hole in her apron. Polly Flinders, who sat among the cinders, did the same thing.

"Oh, we'll get over that," promised the carrot. "Just you watch me!" And really truly, it turned into a rainstorm, and sprinkled down on the flames, and put that fire out. Then, just so Susie wouldn't get wet, the carrot turned into an umbrella; and held itself over her, all the rest of the way home.

So Susie got safely back to the burrow, with all the flowers but the sky-blue-pink one, and she was very happy. And maybe her folks weren't glad too! They had begun to worry about her, and Sammie was just going to start off to look for her. So Susie told how the fairy carrot had brought her home, and Uncle Wiggily said:

"Well, there are certainly queer things happening nowadays. I never would have believed it if you hadn't told me."

"But I have told you," said Susie.

"Ah, well, in that case, of course, I believe you, my dear," said the jolly old rabbit gentleman. And he twinkled his pink nose upside down.

Susie was tired after her adventures with the carrot so she went to bed.

"And that's just where I am going," said Uncle Wiggily.

So the rabbit gentleman tucked himself into bed.

But, in the middle of the night, Nurse Jane Fuzzy Wuzzy was awakened by hearing Susie crying.

"What's the matter?" asked the muskrat lady.

"Oh, I'm so tired I can't seem to go to sleep," said Susie. "I keep thinking about the carrot and my adventures and all that."

"I know what will put you to sleep," said kind Nurse Jane. "I will read you about how, once upon a time, Uncle Wiggily hopped away to look for his fortune. He wrote a book about his search for his fortune. But, as I cannot read you all that book, I will read you from it a few of the stories, just as Uncle Wiggily told them to me."

"Oh, that will be lovely," said Susie.

So, if the postage stamp doesn't jump off the letter and chase the police dog down the street, the next story will be one that Nurse Jane read to Susie Littletail.

STORY XXXII

UNCLE WIGGILY AND THE BEETLE

ONE beautiful sunshiny day, when the wind was blowing through the tree-tops, making music like a church organ many miles away, Uncle Wiggily awakened in the little house which the red monkey had built for him in the deep woods.

"Well, I'm going to make another search for my fortune this morning," Mr. Longears said as he wiggled his whiskers to get the dried leaves out of them; for he had slept on a bed of leaves, you know.

"And I'll go with you," said the red monkey. "Because the last two or three times you hopped off by yourself you got into trouble."

"Trouble? I should say I did!" exclaimed the old gentleman rabbit.

"There was the time when you fell into the can of molasses, and the hippity-hop toad had to jump up and down with it on his back, until it was made into sticks of candy," said the red monkey.

"True enough," spoke Uncle Wiggily.

"And then there was the time when the skillery-scalery alligator chased you," went on the
red monkey, "and the angle worms tied themselves into knots about his legs to stop him. Do
you remember that?"

"Indeed I do," said the old gentleman rabbit.
"And I will be very glad to have you come along
with me and help me. We will start right after
breakfast."

So the two friends built a little camp-fire in
front of the wooden house in the woods and they
cooked some oatmeal and some carrots and turnips, and Uncle Wiggily made a cherry pie with
plenty of red juice in it. And the monkey found
a bag of peanuts under a chestnut tree and he
roasted them for his breakfast. Then they
started off.

On and on they traveled through the woods,
over the hills, up one side and down the other,
around the corner, where a big gray rock rested
on some green moss, and then, all of a sudden,
there was heard a queer noise up in the air. It
was like wings fluttering and a voice calling.
And the voice said:

"Is the red monkey down there?"

"Oh, my! I wonder who can want you?" asked
Uncle Wiggily.

"Maybe it's the bear who once climbed up a tree after me," cried the red monkey. "I'm going to hide." So he crawled under a big, broad leaf where he could not be seen. Then once more the voice called:

"I want the red monkey!"

"Oh, please Uncle Wiggily, don't let him get me!" begged the shivering and shaking monkey. "Throw a stone at that bear, will you?"

"Ha! Hum!" exclaimed the old gentleman rabbit. "I don't very well see how it can be a bear. Bears don't fly in the air, for they have no wings. I'll take a look."

So he looked up in the air, and there, instead of a bear flying overhead, it was only Dickie Chip-Chip, the little sparrow boy.

"Well, bless my pink twinkling nose!" cried Uncle Wiggily. "What are you doing up there, Dickie?"

"Oh, I'm making believe I'm a messenger boy," said the sparrow. "I have a telegram for the red monkey."

"Oh, ho! So that's why you wanted me, is it?" asked the long-tailed chap, as he crawled out from under the leaf. "What is the message about, if you please?"

"Here it is," chirped Dickie, and then from under his wing he took a piece of white cocoanut with writing on it. And no sooner had the red monkey read it than he began to cry.

"What's the matter?" asked Uncle Wiggily.

"Oh, dear!" sobbed the red monkey, "my little brother, who works on a hand organ, nearly had his tail cut off by getting it twisted around the handle. He is very sick, and I must go home right away. Oh, how sorry I am!" and then the red monkey ate up the piece of cocoanut that had the message written on it.

"You had better go home at once," said Uncle Wiggily. .

"But I don't like to leave you," said the red monkey.

"Oh, I will get along all right!" spoke the brave old rabbit gentleman. "Go ahead, and when your brother is well, come back."

"I will," promised the red monkey, as he started for home.

"And I'll fly on ahead to tell them he is coming," said Dickie Chip-Chip. So they both called good-by to Uncle Wiggily, and hurried away through the woods, while the rabbit gentleman kept on in search of his fortune. And now for the black beetle.

Uncle Wiggily was walking along under a green tree, looking for some gold or diamonds when, all of a sudden something jumped out of

the bushes and grabbed his crutch away from
him. Then Uncle Wiggily saw that it was a
wolf, and the wolf sprang down into a big hole
in the ground, taking the crutch with him.

"Now," called the wolf, showing his ugly teeth,
"if you want your crutch, Mr. Rabbit, you'll have
to come down this hole after it. Come on down."

But Uncle Wiggily knew better than that, for
just as surely as he jumped down into that hole
the wolf would have eaten him all up. And the
rabbit didn't know what to do, for he couldn't
walk without his crutch on account of being lame
with the rheumatism.

"Oh, this is terrible!" cried the rabbit. "Whatever shall I do? I can't stay in these woods for-
ever."

And just then there was a rustling in the
leaves, and out walked a big black, pinching
beetle. In front of his head he had two things
just like fire tongs, or a crab's claws, with which
to pinch.

"What is the trouble?" asked the black beetle
politely.

"The wolf, down the hole, has my crutch, and
he won't give it to me," said the rabbit.

"Ha! we will very soon fix that," spoke the
beetle. "Just tie a string around me, Uncle
Wiggily, and lower me down into the hole.

Then I'll pick up the crutch in my strong pincers, and you can haul me up again as I hold fast to it."

"But the wolf may get you," said the rabbit.

"I'll fix that wolf," replied the beetle, winking his two little eyes, real jolly-like.

So Uncle Wiggily tied a string around the black insect, and lowered him down into the hole. The wolf saw him coming and cried out:

"Oh! You can't get this crutch, for I'm sitting on it, and I'll bite you."

"Just you watch," spoke the black beetle, winking one eye this time. So he looked down, and, surely enough, the wolf was sitting on the crutch. But the beetle knew a good trick. He swung himself around on the end of the string, which the rabbit held, and, as he got near to the wolf, the beetle suddenly pinched the savage creature on the tail.

"Oh, my! Ouch!" cried the wolf, and he jumped up in a hurry. And that was just what the beetle wanted, for now he could reach the crutch as the wolf was not sitting on it any more. In his strong pincers the beetle took hold of the crutch.

"Pull me up!" called the beetle to the rabbit, and Uncle Wiggily did so, crutch and all, by the string, and they left the wolf down in the hole as angry as a mud pie.   So that's how the beetle got back the rabbit's crutch for him, and that's the end of this story.

But there'll be another one soon, about Uncle Wiggily and Kittie Kat—that is if the puppy dog across the street doesn't chew a hole in the milk bottle and jiggle the iceman all to pieces so that he goes roller skating with the jumping rope.

"Oh, that was a lovely story," said Susie. "Thank you, Nurse Jane."

"Are you ready to go to sleep now?" asked Miss Fuzzy Wuzzy.

"Oh, no.   Please read me more about how Uncle Wiggily looked for his fortune," begged Susie.

"And I want to hear, too," said Sammie, hopping out of his room.

"Oh, my goodness!   What funny little rabbit children you are," laughed Nurse Jane.   But she read them another story.

STORY XXXIII

UNCLE WIGGILY AND KITTIE KAT

"WELL," said Uncle Wiggily, as he and the black beetle went along through the woods, after the rabbit's crutch had been taken away from the savage wolf, "don't you want to come along with me, Mr. Beetle, and help me look for my fortune?"

"Indeed, I would like to very much," said the funny little insect. "But the truth of the matter is that I have to go to work to-morrow, and so I can't come."

"Work—what work do you do?" inquired Uncle Wiggily.

"Oh, I am going to punch holes in trolley car transfers with my strong pincers," answered the beetle. "Now, I will have to bid you good-by, but if ever any one takes your crutch down a hole again, send for me and I'll get it back for you."

So the beetle said good-by to the old gentleman rabbit, and went his way, and Uncle Wiggily, after looking at his crutch to be sure the wolf had not bitten a piece out of it, hopped on looking for his fortune.

"My! It's quite lonesome going along by myself," said the rabbit, as he hopped through the woods. "I miss the red monkey and the grasshopper and the black beetle. But then they can't always be with me, so I'll have to travel on alone."

On and on he went. Sometimes in the fields he stopped to hear the birds sing, and he heard them talking among themselves about how they must soon get ready to go down South, for cold weather was coming. That made the old gentleman rabbit feel a little sad, and he wished that he could soon go back home, where Sammie and Susie Littletail were waiting for him.

"But I can't go until I find my fortune," he said. "I must look harder than ever for it."

Then, sometimes, when he went through the woods, he heard the little brooks whispering to the ferns, how that soon there would be ice and snow all over, with boys and girls skating and sliding down hill.

"Burr-r-r-r-r-r! That makes me shiver!" exclaimed the rabbit. "I, too, must get ready for winter, Oh, if I could only find that gold and those diamonds for my fortune I'd go right straight home, and never travel about any more."

So he looked under stones and down in hollow stumps, but not a piece of gold nor a sparkling diamond could he find. Then it began to get late, and the sun was darkened behind the clouds.

"I wonder where I can stay to-night?" thought Uncle Wiggily. "I must pick out a nice, big stump, fill it with leaves, and sleep in there."

Well, it didn't take him long to find what he wanted, and he prepared his bed for the night. Then he built a little fire in front of the stump and cooked his supper. He ate some carrots and a turnip sandwich with peanut butter on it, and the last thing he ate was a large piece of cherry pie. Then he washed the dishes and, curling up on the soft leaves, he was soon asleep, dreaming of his little nephew and niece, Sammie and Susie.

Now, about midnight, the savage alligator, who hadn't had anything to eat in a long time, started out to find something. And pretty soon he came to the stump where Uncle Wiggily was sleeping.

"Ah, there is a good meal for me!" cried the skillery-scalery creature, as he reared up on the end of his double-jointed tail and put his long nose down in the hollow stump.

"Hey! What's this? Who is it? Has the red monkey come back?" cried the rabbit, suddenly awakening. "I'm glad to see you, Mr. Monkey. Here is some cherry pie for you."

And then, being only half awake, Uncle Wiggily took a large piece of the pie and held it out, thinking he was giving it to the monkey. But it slipped from his hand and it fell right into the alligator's face.

And the cherry juice ran down into the eyes of the skillery-scalery creature, and tickled him so that he sneezed, and then he ran away, for he thought the red monkey might possibly be in the stump, and the alligator was afraid the monkey might throw hot potatoes down his throat.

Uncle Wiggily looked out of the stump, and by the light of the silvery moon he saw the alligator running away, and that was the first time Mr. Longears knew it was the skillery-scalery creature, and not the monkey, who had come in so suddenly.

"My! That was a narrow escape!" cried the rabbit. "It's a good thing I took that cherry pie to bed with me. I must be on the watch, for the alligator may come back." But the skillery-scalery creature, with the double-jointed tail, didn't return, though Uncle Wiggily didn't sleep very well the rest of the night on account of being so anxious and worrying so much.

And in the morning when he awakened from a

little nap the old gentleman rabbit felt very
strange. He tried to get up, but he found that
he couldn't. He was as dizzy as if he had been
on a merry-go-round and he felt very ill.

"It must have been the fright the alligator
gave me," he thought. "Oh, dear, what shall I
do? Here I am, all alone in this stump in the
woods, and no one to help me. Oh, I'm a poor,
forsaken old rabbit, and nobody loves me! Oh,
if Sammie or Susie were only here. I'm
sure——"

And just then there was a scratching sound
outside the stump.

"Hark! What's that?" whispered the rabbit.
"That must be the alligator coming back to get
me! And I can't even get up to throw some
cherry pie at him. Oh, if the red monkey or the
black beetle would only come!"

Then the scratching noise sounded again, and
Uncle Wiggily was getting so frightened that
he didn't know what to do. And then, all of a
sudden, he saw something white at the top hole
of the stump, and a voice exclaimed:

"Well, if there isn't my dear old Uncle Wiggily! And you are ill, I know you are. I can
tell by the way your nose twinkles."

"Indeed, I am ill," said the poor rabbit, "but

who are you?" For you know he couldn't see
well, as his glasses had fallen off.

"Oh, I am Kittie Kat," said the voice, and
there, surely enough, was a little pussy girl.
She had been away on her summer vacation, and
was just coming back to get ready for school
when she happened to walk through the woods.
There she heard a voice in the stump, and, going
to look, she saw Uncle Wiggily. Kittie Kat was
a cousin to Katy the pussy who thought the **Katy**
Dids talked about her.

"Oh, how glad I am to see you, Kittie Kat,"
said the rabbit.

"And how sorry I am to see you ill," said the
pussy girl. "But don't worry. I'm going to
make you well. Just keep quiet."

Then that brave little pussy girl scurried
around, and gathered some leaves from a plant
called catnip.

"For," said Kittie, "if catnip is good for cats,
it must be good for rabbits." So she made some
hot catnip tea, and gave it to Uncle Wiggily, and
in an hour he was all better and could sit up.
Then Kittie made him some toast with some
slices of yellow carrots on it, and he felt better
still, and by noon he was as good as ever.

"But I don't know what I would have done,

only for you, Kittie Kat," said the rabbit.
"Thank you, very much. Now I can travel on
and seek my fortune."

"And I'll come with you," spoke Kittie Kat.
So they traveled on together, and they had an
adventure the next day. I'll tell you about it
right away, for the next story will be of Uncle
Wiggily and Jennie Chipmunk—that is, if the
roller skate up in the attic doesn't go off on a
vacation all by itself down to Asbury Grove,
and hide in the sand to fool the popcorn man.

No sooner had Nurse Jane finished the story
than a knock sounded on the door.

"Who is there?" asked Nurse Jane.

"It is I, Uncle Wiggily," was the answer. "I
heard you reading to Sammie and Susie Littletail
to get them to sleep. But you must be tired, Miss
Fuzzy Wuzzy. So I will read the next story
about my fortune."

"Oh, goodie!" said Sammie and Susie.

So Uncle Wiggily took the book and read to
the Littletails this next story.

STORY XXXIV

UNCLE WIGGILY AND JENNIE

"Now, Uncle Wiggily," said Kittie Kat, as she and the old gentleman rabbit went along, the day after he had been cured by the catnip tea, "you must take good care of yourself. Keep in the shade, and walk slowly, for I don't want you to get sick again."

"And I don't want to myself," spoke Uncle Wiggily, "for I want to find my fortune."

"Oh, I think you will, and very soon," said Kittie. "I dreamed last night of a pile of gold and diamonds, and I'm sure you will soon be rich, so that you can come back home, and live with us all again."

"Where was the pile of gold of which you dreamed?" asked the rabbit. "Was it at the end of the rainbow? Because, if it was, there is no use to think of it. I once looked there and found nothing."

"No, it wasn't there," said Kittie, shaking her head. "I don't know where it was because I

181

awakened before my dream was over, but I'm sure you will soon find your fortune. Now remember to walk slowly, and keep in the shade."

So she and Uncle Wiggily traveled on and on. Once they came to a big hill, which they could hardly climb, and they didn't know what to do. But they happened to meet a friendly mud turtle, who was very strong, and who had a large, broad shell.

"Get on my back," said the turtle, "and I will take you up the hill. I go slowly, but I am very sure. You will have time to rest yourselves while I am climbing up."

So Uncle Wiggily and Kittie Kat got on the turtle's back, and in time he took them up the hill. Then, after traveling on a little farther, they came to a broad river.

"Oh, how shall we ever get across?" asked Kittie.

"Perhaps I can make a boat," said the rabbit. He was looking for some wood to make the boat and some broad leaves with which to make a sail, when along came swimming a big goldfish.

"Just perch upon my back," the fish said, "and I will be very glad to take you across."

"But you swim under water, and we will get all wet," objected Uncle Wiggily.

"No, I will swim with my back away up out

of water," said the goldfish, and this he did, so
that the rabbit and the pussy girl were taken
safely over to the other side of the river and they
never even so much as wet their eyelashes.

"Perhaps I may find my fortune over here,"
spoke Uncle Wiggily, as he hopped along after
thanking the goldfish. He looked on the ground,
and up in the air, but no fortune could he find.

"There is a little house, made of leaves and
bark over that way," said Kittie, pointing
through the woods. "Let us go and see who is in
it."

"Perhaps a bear lives there," said the rabbit.

"It is too small for a bear's house," decided
Kittie.

But as they came close to it they heard a
scratching noise inside, and they thought perhaps
it might be the fuzzy fox. And then, all of a
sudden, they heard a voice singing this song:

"I sweep, I sew, I dust, I mend,
    From morning until night.
And then I wash the plates and cups.
    And scrub the table white.

"I love to make a pudding,
    Also a pie and cake.
And when I do my ironing,
    Potatoes do I bake.

"Now I must hurry—hurry,
    To get a meal for you,
And then I'll go and gather
    A hickory nut or two."

"Why, I know who that is!" cried Kittie Kat.

"Who?" asked Uncle Wiggily, making his nose twinkle like three stars and a moon on a frosty night.

"It's Jennie Chipmunk!" cried Kittie. "I just know it is. Oh, Jennie!" she called. "Is that you?"

"Yes, who is it that wants me?" asked a voice, and out from the tiny house stepped the little chipmunk girl. She had on her sweeping cap, and her apron, and in one hand was a cloth and in the other a plate she was drying.

"Well, well, Jennie, you're as busy as ever, I see!" exclaimed Uncle Wiggily. "But are you living here?"

"Hush! No," answered Jennie Chipmunk. "I don't live here, but in this house is a dear old lady squirrel, who is so feeble that she can't get around and do all her work. So every day I come over and clean up for her, and get her meals. Oh, I just love to work!" cried Jennie.

"I believe you," spoke the rabbit. "But can't we help?"

"Of course we can," decided Kittie. "You get some wood for the fire, Uncle Wiggily, and Jennie and I will do the housework."

Then the rabbit and Kittie went in the little house, and Jennie Chipmunk introduced them to the old lady squirrel, who had to lie down in bed most of the time.

"Oh, I am very glad to see you," she said in her gentle voice. "I don't know what I would do without Jennie. She is such a help; aren't you, Jennie?"

But Jennie wasn't there to answer, for she had skipped out into the kitchen to finish the dishes, and she was singing away as she hurried along as happy as a grasshopper.

Then Uncle Wiggily brought in a lot of wood, and with Kittie to help with the sweeping and dusting, the house was soon as neat as a piece of apple pie on a Sunday morning.

"Oh, thank you, ever so much," said the old lady squirrel. "Thank you, Jennie. And thank you, Uncle Wiggily. And I hope you will soon find your fortune."

"Thank you," said Uncle Wiggily. "I am going to start out again, soon, to seek my fortune. Perhaps I may take the Littletails with me. That is I will if they can stay awake and do not fall—do not—do not fall a—a—asleep—er—"

Then, all of a sudden, the book from which he was reading fell from his paw, and Uncle Wiggily fell asleep. His pink nose stopped twinkling.

And Nurse Jane was asleep.

And Sammie was asleep.

And Susie was asleep.

They were all asleep.

And the next morning— Oh, but there is no more room in this book for any stories; not even for Uncle Wiggily to read to the Littletails.

But in another book I am going to put some new stories—all about how Uncle Wiggily found his fortune and about his wonderful adventures.

But now we must let Uncle Wiggily and the Littletails and Nurse Jane sleep quietly. For tomorrow will be another day.

THE END

5 M